GIRLS
TO THE
RESCUE
BOOK #4

*Tales of clever, courageous girls
from around the world*

EDITED BY BRUCE LANSKY

Meadowbrook Press
Distributed by Simon & Schuster
New York

Library of Congress Catalog Card Number: 95-17733

Publisher's ISBN: 0-88166-301-8
Simon & Schuster Ordering # 0-671-57703-4

Editor: Bruce Lansky
Editorial Coordinator: Liya Lev Oertel
Copyeditor: Christine Walske
Production Manager: Joe Gagne
Production Assistant: Danielle White
Cover Illustrator: Joy Allen

© 1998 by Meadowbrook Creations

p. 1, "Fishing for Trouble" © 1997 by Sandy Cudmore; p. 13 "Rachel's Promise" © 1997 by Liya Lev Oertel; p. 25 "Keesha and the Rat!" © 1997 by Jack Kelly; p. 33 "Temper, Temper" © 1997 by Bruce Lansky; p. 49 "Skateboard Rosie and the Soda Kids" © 1997 by Diane Sawyer; p. 67 "Save Wellington Woods!!" © 1997 by Laurie Eynon; p. 79 "The Apple Pie House" © 1997 by Janet Smith; p. 93 "Mai's Magic" © 1997 by Jason Sanford

Published by Meadowbrook Press, 5451 Smetana Drive; Minnetonka, MN 55343

BOOK TRADE DISTRIBUTION by Simon & Schuster, a division of Simon and Schuster, Inc., 1230 Avenue of the Americas, New York, NY 10020

02 01 00 99 98   12 11 10 9 8 7 6 5 4 3 2 1

Printed in the United States of America

Dedication

This book is dedicated to my daughter, Dana. I used to make up stories for her when she was young, hoping to inspire her to believe in herself and to pursue her dreams. It is in that spirit that I have written and collected the stories in this series.

Acknowledgments

Thank you to all the young women who served
on a reading panel for this project:

Stephanie Adams, Michelle Anthony, Tiffany Ascensio, Sarah
Ashley, Ana Bascuñan, Jennifer Bohall, Lauren Borkowski,
Valerie Breault, Jody Burch, Ashley Collier, Cara Cooper,
Stephanie Conroy, Amanda Dameron, Ashlie Dufour, Jennifer
Durham, JaNeese Ellis, Sarah Erni, Jasmine Falta, Amy
Finnerty, Kimberly Fleming, Audrey Fresquez, Roberta
Georgerian, Laura Goulding, Jenny Guptill, Emma Gutelius,
Bethany Harrison, Haley Hastings, Claire Helring, Vanessa
Hoza, Jennifer Kensok, Courtney Lang, Marissa Lingo, Audrey
Logan, Amanda Longley, Tracy Matzdorf, Merit McCrea,
Denise McCullough, Ashley Moch, Angela Moore, Ashley
Nobles, Melissa N. Pleiss, Jamie Radford, Kiera Reinsch, Stephie
Ruch, Jo Ellen Rutherford, Stacy Sanok, Stephanie Silver,
Meagan Smith, Sarah Stock, Lauren Stone, Bailey Summers,
Sally Tucker, Jennifer Volk, Ashley Wallace, Natalie Watkins,
Melissa Whitfield, Domonique Williams, Emily Winters, Ashley
Witherwax, Meggie Wittorf

Contents

Introduction

Our first *Girls to the Rescue* book contained ten stories set in a time when monsters, trolls, and unicorns roamed the earth and Cinderella was a big crybaby.

The stories in this book are very different: they take place in the twentieth century. They are stories about clever, courageous girls (just like you) from all around the world:

- a quick-thinking cousin from a small town in Mississippi
- a clever farmer's daughter from Italy
- a spunky sister from Harlem
- an environmental activist from Ontario
- a stealthy sleuth from Thailand
- a pastry cook from Venezuela
- a responsible sister from Russia
- a daredevil skateboarder from Tampa Bay

If you're like the sixty girls who helped us select these stories, I think you'll enjoy them as much as the stories in the first book, the second, and the third.

If you haven't read the first three books in the *Girls to the Rescue* series, you've got a lot to look forward to. And if you're wondering about the fifth book, I want you to know that we're working on it as fast as we can. It should be out in the fall of 1998 (if all goes well).

Bruce Lansky

FISHING FOR TROUBLE

AN ORIGINAL STORY BY SANDY CUDMORE

"Middle of Nowhere, Mississippi—I can't believe I have to spend my whole spring break here instead of back in L.A.," complained Gabe. "This place is— what—twenty miles from the nearest town? Tunica? What kind of dumb name is Tunica?"

"It's Native American, after the Tunica tribe," said Kayla. She sat in the den with her new—what was he? Her stepcousin? Kayla's favorite uncle, Dan, had recently married Gabe's mom out in California. Gabe was thirteen, same as Kayla. Their age was all they had in common so far.

They'd already gone through Kayla's whole collection of video games. Gabe had easily won them all.

"These games are lame. And you couldn't even get to level two of that last one. I could beat that game when I was ten," Gabe said. "Let's go to an arcade, where they'll have something with a challenge."

"Tunica doesn't have an arcade. You'd have to drive all the way back to Memphis, where you flew in," said Kayla. "We could go skateboarding."

"That's dumb—skateboarding on a bumpy road with no curbs. No thanks," said Gabe. "Back home, I practice on ramps built for competition."

"We could get some worms and go fishing," suggested Kayla. "I have my own fishing boat."

"Right—as if I'm interested in drowning worms in a dinky little lake," Gabe said. "If they teach geography in Tunica, you'll remember that California is on the Pacific Ocean. My dad and I go deep-sea fishing in a trawler."

Why don't you spend your vacation with him, then? Kayla wanted to blurt out. Instead she asked, "So, your dad lives in L.A., too?"

"Yeah. He's on an important business trip. That's why I got stuck here."

If Gabe weren't such a know-it-all, Kayla might almost feel sorry for him. It didn't sound as if his parents had much time for him. Then again, if he acted like this all the time, she could see why they'd ship him off. She stood. "Well, I'm going fishing. You can come if you want to."

Kayla got her tackle box, two fishing rods, two life jackets, and a coffee can. Gabe followed her to a shady spot alongside the house. Kayla put down her gear and grabbed a shovel that was leaning against the wall. She stepped on the shovel blade and turned over a chunk of muddy earth.

"Here's one," Kayla said. She held out a long, squirming brown worm.

Gabe stared at her. "What?"

"Put it in the can," Kayla said.

"Why?" he asked, but he took the worm and dropped it into the can.

"So you can take some pets back to California! They're the bait, Einstein. Here's another," she said.

"When my dad and I go fishing, we *buy* our bait at the marina," Gabe said.

"Well, Moon Lake doesn't have a marina, so we *dig* ours up," said Kayla.

When the can was stuffed with dirt and fat, twisting worms, Kayla wiped her hands on the grass and then on the back of her pants. Then she picked up the fishing gear, and Gabe followed her to the lake. As they passed the kitchen door, Kayla stuck her head in.

"Mom, we're taking the boat and going fishing. . . . Got 'em," she yelled, holding up the two life jackets.

Gabe followed her down the slippery bank. Kayla stood in the mucky water and loaded the equipment. Gabe pointed at the little mud stacks poking up all around.

"What are those?" he asked.

"Crawdad holes. You can get in the boat. Sit in the middle. I'll push us off," she said. She could tell he didn't want to wade in the mud.

"Do they bite?" he asked.

"Naw, but they'll pinch. Some people eat 'em. Crawdad stew."

"That's dumb," Gabe said, looking around in disgust.

Kayla smirked as she untied the boat. "City kid," she thought. "Dumb, dumb, dumb—that's his favorite word." She stepped deeper into the water, shoved the boat, and climbed in. The little aluminum boat rocked wildly as she climbed in the back.

"Hey!" Gabe yelled, holding both sides.

"You don't get seasick, do you?" Kayla grinned.

"Not usually. But I don't want to go swimming with those crawdads, thank you."

"Never flipped it yet," Kayla said. "By the way, there are water moccasins in this lake, too."

"Snakes, great," Gabe muttered.

"They can't get you unless you fall in."

She tugged the starter rope of her five-horse Johnson. It started on the second pull. As they bounced across the choppy waves, the bait can tipped over. Worms crawled all over the bottom of the boat. Kayla scooped them up and shoved them back in the can with both hands.

"Hey, who's driving this thing?" Gabe yelled over the motor's noise.

"Nobody," Kayla said. She leaned over the side to wash her muddy hands.

"Don't you look where you're going?" he asked.

"Why? You see any other boats?"

Gabe looked around. "No. Where is everybody? In California, there'd be two hundred boats out here."

"Not in Mississippi. Maybe ten or twelve boats on a busy day. On a Monday in April, we'll have the whole lake to ourselves," said Kayla. "We just need to keep an eye out for storms. They come up quick this time of year."

The shoreline was covered with cypress trees, tall grasses, and ferns. Kayla turned the boat shoreward and cut the motor. They glided in under the trees. She reached up for a low-hanging branch and stopped the boat by holding on.

Two turtles were sleeping on a cypress root. They looked up, slipped into the water, and disappeared.

"Well, *excuse* us," Gabe said loudly, as if yelling over the motor.

"Sshh," whispered Kayla. "You'll scare away the fish."

She held the line of one of the rods between her knees, with the hook poking up. Gabe did the same. Then she pulled a worm out of the can. She made a few quick bends in the worm and poked the hook through. After she quietly rinsed her hand in the water, she cast out her line. Gabe picked up a worm and held it near his hook. He tried to poke the hook through it, then put the worm back in the can and dropped his rod to the bottom of the boat.

"So this is how country kids have fun, huh?" he asked.

Kayla ignored him. Her red-and-white bobber ducked under the water. She cranked the reel and pulled out a shiny flapping fish.

"A good-size brim," Kayla said. "Grab it."

She maneuvered the fish up over the boat. Gabe took hold of the line about a foot from the fish. It flopped around and smacked him in the face.

"Yuck," he said. He wiped his face on his sleeve. "This is so dumb. Let's go exploring or something."

Kayla grabbed the fish, pulled the hook free from its mouth, and tossed it back in the lake. It lay stunned on its side for a second, then swam away.

"Okay. We can explore the lake some if you want," Kayla said. "There's an island across from here."

"Move over. I want to drive," said Gabe.

"I guess that'd be all right," she said. "Do you know how to drive a boat?"

"What's to know? If you can do it, I certainly can," he said.

They traded seats, and Gabe drove the boat to the other side of the lake. Kayla pointed to a graceful white heron at the edge of the water.

Gabe shrugged. "Aren't there any Jet Skis on this lake?" he asked.

"Not this time of year," Kayla said. She looked at the sky behind Gabe. "We better get home. Weather's comin.'"

"What do you mean?"

"Storm clouds," she said.

"Who's afraid of a black cloud?" Gabe asked.

"Storms come up quick. You don't want to be stuck out on the lake when one hits," Kayla said. "Head toward the silver thing on that shore. It's the roof of our barn. And here—put on your life jacket."

"I don't need a life jacket," Gabe said. He dropped his in the bottom of the boat. They started back across the lake. The sky was abruptly turning dark. The boat rocked in the whitecaps.

"Point the bow into the waves," Kayla called.

"No, I'll go straight. We'll get back quicker," he said.

The next wave washed over the side of the boat. They sat in ankle-deep water. When the next wave hit, the boat almost capsized. The engine sputtered and stalled.

"Why didn't you listen to me?" Kayla yelled.

"Well, if you didn't have such a dinky boat!" Gabe shouted over a clap of thunder.

"Let me see if I can get it to start," Kayla called. As

they stood up to change seats, rain began to pound them. Another big wave crashed into the boat. Gabe fell, and his face crashed into the bench seat in front. A lot of water had come in. Kayla dumped the worms overboard and started bailing with the coffee can. With her other hand she tugged on the starter rope, but the motor just gurgled.

"It must have gotten swamped when the last wave hit," Kayla called into the wind. She looked at Gabe for the first time since they'd changed seats. He was holding his face, and both his hands were covered with blood. The bridge of his nose was already turning color. Kayla remembered when their mule had kicked her dad in the face and broken his nose. He had looked just like that. Gabe needed to get to a hospital.

Lightning sliced the sky, and thunder crashed around them. Kayla pulled off her shoes, grabbed the rope from the bottom of the boat, and jumped into the water. She knotted the rope to the waist strap of her life jacket and swam toward a small island nearby. When she was able to stand, Kayla towed the boat to shore and pulled it up on the sand. A funnel cloud was moving toward them from across the lake.

"Come on, run!" she yelled. She held Gabe's hand

and they ran up the beach to a grassy knoll. At the top a lip jutted out over the beach. Kayla pulled Gabe down. "Stay as flat as you can! Dig in your fingers!"

They pressed their faces into the dirt. The wind pelted them with grit and grass. Hailstones pounded their backs and legs. The wind alternately pushed them against the ground and tried to drag them away. They pressed themselves as low as they could.

Then as suddenly as the storm had come, it was gone, a ghostly blanket blowing away across the lake.

"Your boat's gone," Gabe said when he looked at the empty shore below.

Kayla looked down the shoreline. The aluminum boat was smashed on some large rocks. Trees were pulled out and branches were everywhere.

"What the heck was that?" Gabe said.

"They don't teach you about tornadoes in California?" Kayla asked.

She found her tackle box on the rocks near her wrecked boat. She used her pocketknife to cut off a section of her pants leg, then soaked the denim in the lake.

"Lean against the bank," Kayla said. She pressed the roll of denim against Gabe's bleeding nose. He winced at the pressure. Next she made a horizontal slice in her T-shirt. She tugged, and the bottom third of her shirt ripped away. She shivered. Higher up the bank, Kayla saw a paddle from her boat. She got it and tied the strip of fabric from her shirt onto one end of the paddle.

"Mom will be watching for us," she said. She stood next to Gabe and waved her T-shirt flag high in the air.

Gabe took the compress away from his nose.

"If it weren't for you, I'd be dead out there in the lake," he said. His nose dribbled two streams of blood.

"You better put that back on your nose," Kayla said. She kept waving her flag.

"I'm serious, Kayla. I had no idea what to do," he said.

"Hey, look over there across the lake!" Kayla exclaimed. "That's our ski boat heading this way. My mom and dad must have seen the flag." She waved the flag to let her parents know she saw them. "I'm glad the tornado didn't wreck our ski boat. Who knows . . . you might have to come back here in the summer."

"I'd like that," Gabe said quietly. "Would you teach me how to ski?"

"Oh sure," Kayla said. "You want *me*, a dumb country girl, to teach *you* something?"

"I'm sorry," Gabe said. "I know I was a real jerk."

"Come on." Kayla helped Gabe up, and they walked down the bank to wait for the boat.

"I mean it," Gabe insisted. "You really saved my life. And you know how to do more stuff than any of my friends at home. Like putting a worm on a hook—I didn't know how to do that." Blood ran down and dropped off his lip.

"Well, I guess I know a lot of stuff about Mississippi," Kayla said thoughtfully. "But I'd be pretty lost in L.A.—you'd be the expert on that!"

"You'd do fine," Gabe told her. "Maybe sometime you could come out and visit. I'd show you around."

Kayla looked at him. "That would be fun." Then she smiled. "I guess you aren't such a big jerk after all."

"Yah . . . well," Gabe mumbled, embarrassed. "I just want us to be friends."

"Friends it is, then," said Kayla. She reached out her hand.

Gabe smiled with relief. "Friends," he said as he reached out to take Kayla's hand.

Rachel's Promise

An Original Story by Liya Lev Oertel

Russian Words:
Ruble (pronounced "ROO-bel"): Russian money.
Nyet: means "no."

Yiddish Word:
Latke (pronounced "LAHT-keh"): small pancake, usually made out of grated potatoes.

Rachel was five when her sister Ida was born. Rachel was a shy, quiet girl. She could sit for hours outside their wooden house in the small Russian village, playing with flowers and drawing pictures in the dirt. When her mother, Sarah, told her that she would soon have a little sister, Rachel wasn't sure whether this was good news. As the months passed, she watched her mother's tummy grow and wondered how her life would change.

Then, one day, Sarah went to the hospital in a neighboring town. She returned a week later.

"Rachel," Sarah called, "come and meet your sister."

Rachel was worried. After all, she had been perfectly happy for five years. Why did she need a sister? But the minute Rachel saw Ida's big eyes and round cheeks, she changed her mind.

"Well, Rachel, what do you think?" asked Sarah with a smile.

"She is beautiful, Mama," whispered Rachel. "Can I touch her?"

"Of course," Rachel's mother said. "Just be careful. She is very small and very fragile. So you'll have to be a good big sister and protect her. Will you do that, Rachel?"

"I will," Rachel solemnly promised. In fact, then and there she promised herself that she would always do her best to keep her little sister happy and protect her from all the hurts of the world.

As the years passed, Ida grew into a plump, cheerful girl with dimples and a ready smile. Rachel grew tall, skinny, and serious. She had always kept her promise and always protected Ida from anything that might erase her smile. Rachel chased away the boys who tried to pull Ida's braids, even though she would never have had the courage to stand up for herself. She helped Ida with her chores, and she saved the tastiest morsels of cake and the crispiest potato latkes for her little sister.

When Rachel started school, she would come home and show Ida what she learned. When Ida was old enough to go to school herself, the sisters walked hand in hand to the one-room village schoolhouse. In the evenings, Rachel helped Ida with her homework.

In the summer the sisters ran barefoot in the fields surrounding their little village, playing games and picking flowers. They wore simple, faded dresses and never worried about getting dirty. Their dresses had already been washed and mended so many times, they knew one more wash wouldn't hurt them. Rachel had only two dresses—a plain one for every day and a pretty, new one for special occasions. Ida wore Rachel's hand-me-downs. The girls never thought about their clothes, because all the village children dressed the same way.

When Rachel was fourteen and Ida was nine, their parents decided to move away from their village. Their father, Isaac, had a brother in the big city of Minsk who had been writing about all the wonders of the city and the opportunities that were not available in the small village. Sarah was a nurse at the tiny village clinic, and she hoped to find a more exciting job at a big, modern hospital. Isaac was a veterinarian, and he hoped to get a job at the city zoo.

They packed their few belongings and moved to Minsk. Since they had little money and did not know anyone else, they moved in with Isaac's brother and his wife. The apartment was small, so the whole family slept in one room. The girls soon enrolled in the neighborhood school, and Isaac and Sarah began looking for work.

City life was not as rosy as Isaac's brother had described. Wonderful jobs did not come knocking on their door. No one wanted a village nurse, and the zoo already had all the veterinarians it needed. Isaac and Sarah spent long days walking door to door, employment agency to employment agency, hoping to find some work.

Meanwhile, Rachel and Ida were having a hard

time in their new school. They had to go to separate classes and meet new children. After school, Rachel waited for Ida, and they walked home together. But they didn't run or play games or laugh as they used to. They were unaccustomed to all the cars on the roads and all the people on the sidewalks, so they had to walk slowly and carefully.

The worst of it all was their clothing. They wore the same old dresses they'd worn back in the village. But the other kids seemed to wear different clothes almost every day. Rachel's classmates made fun of her one dress, and although Ida never mentioned anything, Rachel knew that she got teased as well.

Rachel watched Ida's smile grow dimmer and more uncertain, and she saw her looking wistfully into the windows of the clothing shops they passed on the way to and from school. This was the first time Rachel couldn't keep her promise—she could do nothing to protect her little sister from the mean kids and she could not bring a smile to Ida's face. As Ida saddened, so did she. Rachel knew that her parents barely had enough money to pay for their share of the apartment and food, and what little money they had was running out fast. She couldn't possibly ask them for new clothes.

After school, the girls would come directly home and do their homework and whatever chores they had for the day. Afterward they sat at the window of their crowded room in the second-story apartment. The window faced the street, and the sisters spent hours watching the people below. They especially liked to admire the girls' outfits. Ida made a game out of choosing a favorite outfit or creating one out of pieces worn by different girls.

"Rachel, look at the girl with the long, dark hair!" Ida would exclaim. "Isn't her gray sweater pretty? I think it would go so nicely with that green skirt the blond girl on the corner is wearing, don't you? And look over there, the girl with the ponytail: isn't her blue dress wonderful?" During this game, Ida again became her cheerful self. She laughed, showing her dimples, and her eyes sparkled.

Rachel would look at the girl Ida pointed out and agree that the sweater was pretty and the dress was wonderful. Then she would look at her sister's worn dress and think how pretty Ida would look in that blue dress.

Rachel often thought about getting something pretty for her sister. She would have gladly given Ida her one good dress, but it was too big for Ida. The skirt came down to the floor, the top was too roomy, and the sleeves were much too long.

Then one day she had a great idea: she would cut her dress in half and make a new skirt and blouse for Ida. She could cut some material off both ends of the skirt to make it shorter. She could shorten the sleeves to fit Ida's arms. And she could remove some material from the back of the blouse and then sew it up again. How hard could this be? Rachel could already imagine Ida wearing her new outfit and being admired by everybody.

One day when Rachel was alone in the apartment, she decided to put her plan into action. She took her good dress out of the closet and spread it lovingly on the floor. Then she brought a pair of scissors from the kitchen, took one last look at her dress, took a deep breath, and cut the dress in half along the waist. Then she went to work—cutting, measuring, frowning, and cutting some more.

Finally Rachel stopped and examined her handiwork. To her dismay, it was not at all what she'd envisioned. The cuts were crooked; her first one ran not along the waist, but almost from one armpit to the opposite hip. The part of the dress that used to be the skirt looked nothing like a skirt at all, but more like a long piece of fabric sewn together at the shorter ends. The sleeves were different lengths, one cut almost to the elbow. And the rest of the top! Well, that was unrecognizable.

"What have I done?" Rachel whispered in horror, holding up the rags she'd created. Not only had she failed to make Ida happy, but she'd also ruined her only nice dress. What would her parents say?

Rachel's parents came home tired and worried, as usual. When they saw what she had done, they were very angry.

"How could you do this, Rachel?" Sarah asked wearily. Sarah was so upset, she began to cry. "You know we have no money, and now you've ruined your only good dress. Who knows when we will be able to buy you another?"

Rachel cried too—but not about ruining the dress. That wasn't important. She cried because she'd made her mother unhappy. She couldn't bear to think that she'd added to her mother's troubles.

"Oh, Mama, I am so sorry," Rachel cried. "Please don't be upset." She ran to hug her mother. "Don't worry. I don't mind not having another dress. I just wanted to make something nice for Ida."

Rachel sobbed herself to sleep that night in the bed she shared with Ida. She covered her head with her pillow so Ida wouldn't hear. She cried because she'd made her mother unhappy. She cried because she missed her village. And most of all, she cried because she couldn't keep the promise she'd made so long ago to keep her little sister happy.

For the next few weeks, Rachel was even quieter than usual. She kept the ruined dress in the closet and looked at it every day. Then she had an idea.

During the following weeks, Rachel and Ida did not go home right after school. Instead, they went to the library. Rachel would find some fun books for Ida to read while she pored over sewing books and dress patterns. The girls ignored the children who pointed at their worn dresses and laughed at the "village bumpkins," and paid no attention to those who called out, "Hey, what are you doing in here? The library has no cows for you to milk!"

Rachel read all the sewing books in the library, using dictionaries to understand the technical words. In the evening, she sat in a corner of her family's room and experimented with fabric from the ruined dress. Eventually, she used a few of these scraps to make a dress for Ida's doll—a really fancy dress with pockets and ruffles and bows.

Ida was very proud of her sister and the beautiful dress she'd made. The next day, Ida actually looked forward to going to school. She brought her doll with her and showed it to her classmates.

When Rachel met her sister after school, she saw that for the first time since they had come to Minsk Ida was smiling.

"Rachel," Ida shouted excitedly, "listen! Three girls in my class asked if you could make doll dresses for them, too! Can you, Rachel? Please? They were so nice to me. No one laughed at me today."

"Sure," Rachel answered, smiling at Ida's smile. "I would be happy to, as long as I have enough fabric."

Rachel used up the rest of the ruined dress on two more doll dresses, which Ida proudly brought to school and gave to two of the girls in her class.

"What about me?" asked the third girl.

"My sister would be glad to make one for you too," Ida told her, "but she has run out of fabric."

The next day, the girl gave Ida a few rubles. "Here,"

she said. "Give these to your sister. She can buy enough fabric for the dress. If any money is left over, she can keep it."

And so it went. Word of Rachel's talent spread all over the school, and all the girls wanted Rachel to sew clothes for their dolls. The girls' parents gave Rachel money to buy fabric and told her to keep any extra money. And there was always a little left over.

The more Rachel sewed, the faster and better she became. She scoured magazines for ideas and began creating her own designs. She loved being good at something, and with her new confidence, she made many friends. She kept all the money she made in an old shoebox.

At first she tried to give the money to her parents. But Isaac refused to take it.

"*Nyet,* Rachel," Isaac told her. "Thank you, but we don't want to take your money. You've worked hard for it, so you keep it and buy yourself something nice."

After six months, Rachel took out the shoebox, counted her money, and smiled. That weekend she told Ida to look through magazines in the library and choose the outfit she would most like to have. Ida looked and looked—everything looked so pretty!

Finally Ida chose a long, narrow denim skirt and a sky-blue blouse. Rachel took Ida to the fabric store, and together they picked out fabric for the new outfit.

Every evening that week, Rachel worked on the skirt and blouse. Now she knew what to do. Her cuts were straight and sure, and her stitching was neat. She measured Ida carefully to make sure everything would fit. She was finished on Sunday and lay the skirt and blouse on the bed.

"Ida, come into the bedroom," she called. "I am finished."

Ida ran into the bedroom, her eyes shining. "Where, where, let me see!" When she saw the finished outfit, she clapped her hands and threw her arms around Rachel's neck. "They're beautiful!" she exclaimed, dancing around the room with her new clothes. "They're even prettier than in the picture. Oh, Rachel, thank you! You are the best sister anyone could ever have." Ida tried on her new outfit right away. It fit perfectly.

As they walked to school the next morning, Rachel looked proudly at her little sister, whose smile lit up the whole street. Rachel had kept her promise after all.

Keesha
and the Rat

AN ORIGINAL STORY BY J.M. KELLY

My name is Keesha, and I am proud to be an African-American girl. I am proud to live in Harlem, and I am proud to be in the fifth grade at Sojourner Truth Elementary School. Did I tell you our school took first place in the New York City Math-Science Tournament? Well, we did, and I was on the team.

I love my mama, I love my baby brother, I love my neighborhood, and I love my friends. But there's one thing I don't love—rats.

Our apartment is kind of small. My mama keeps it clean, but she can't do much about some things. The windows need fixing and the hallways need painting. But the rats are worst of all. I am always worrying: Is a rat going to sneak into my bed? Is a rat going to bite my little brother Raymond?

One time a rat was sneaking along the wall right toward Raymond's crib. I had to throw a shoe at it—I don't like to get anywhere near rats.

Then I went to Mama and said, "Mama, we have to do something about these rats. They're all over the neighborhood. Why do we have to live with rats?"

"We're poor, Keesha," she said. Mama is a sales clerk at a big store downtown. She doesn't make much money, and she and my dad are divorced.

"I know we're poor, but I don't think that's any kind of reason. I'm writing a letter to the City. I'm telling them they have to get up here and do something."

"You do that, girl," Mama said. "You go right ahead and do it."

And I did it. Then I waited. A letter came back in a fancy envelope that said "City of New York." All right!

I opened it up. It said, "Thank you for your interest." My interest? That's all? Why are they thanking me for my interest? Why aren't they doing something about these rats?

I called up the commissioner of housing. A lady answered the telephone and said, "Can I help you?"

"Rats," I said. "R-A-T-S, rats!"

"We'll send you a form," the lady said. Sure enough, a few days later, the form showed up in our mailbox. I filled it out, told all about the rats, and sent it back. Then I waited some more. Nothing happened.

"I'm going down there to talk to them," I told Mama.

"Keesha, honey, when you get an idea in your head, you don't give up, do you?" She smiled and I felt good.

Mama went down to the commissioner's office with me. She had to take time off from work, but she was glad to do it.

The woman at the desk told us we had to wait to see the commissioner. So we waited, and waited, and waited. Finally the commissioner came out of his office.

I jumped up. "I want to talk to you. We have rats!"

"I suggest you fill out a form," he said, hurrying out the door. "Or better yet, send a letter."

"But wait a minute," I said. He didn't wait a minute or even a second. He was out the door.

Well! That made me pretty mad. I made up my mind to do something about those rats one way or another.

Then I got lucky. I found out that every once in a while, the mayor visited schools in the city. Guess where he was visiting on Monday? That's right: Harlem—Sojourner Truth Elementary.

I got an idea. I decided to catch a real, live rat and take it to school to show Mr. Mayor just what we had to live with. Maybe he didn't even know how ugly and mean rats were. He had to see these monsters himself. Then he'd want to do something about them.

After church on Sunday I found a white ice-cream pail and poked some air holes in it. I found a board to put on top of it and a stick to prop up the board and a string to tie to the stick. I put some cheese inside the pail and set the trap in the corner of Raymond's and my bedroom where I'd seen the rats.

Now, our apartment has cracks that run along the walls and down along the floor. As I watched one of those cracks, sure enough—I saw a rat. First I saw its nose sniffing around. Then I saw its beady black eyes peering out. Then I watched it squeeze its ugly self right through the crack and creep along the floor.

But I didn't move. That rat was planning on having a nice snack, and I didn't want to scare it off. I could see its yellow teeth and its long, yucky tail. Ugh!

The rat was suspicious at first. It sniffed here and there, its little whiskers twitching. But it couldn't resist and climbed right into the pail to get the cheese. I pulled the string. *Bam!* I got it.

I didn't want to go near that pail, but I did. I lifted the board a crack and slipped the pail's lid on and tied it down. Then I tied it again, just to make sure old Cheese-Breath couldn't get out.

The next day I took the rat to school. Its constant scratching gave me shivers up my spine. I would rather have been doing just about anything other than carrying a rat around, believe me. But I was not turning back now.

Our teacher, Mrs. Perez, told us we all had to be really good so we would make a good impression on the mayor. But I thought he should make a good impression on us by doing his job.

Finally, the mayor and a bunch of other people came crowding into our classroom. And who was there with them, big as life? The commissioner of housing. Of course, he didn't even recognize me.

The mayor talked to Mrs. Perez about what we were studying. I was getting nervous. This was the mayor of the whole city. I was just a ten-year-old girl.

He started asking us what we thought about school and all. I knew this was my one chance. I raised my hand.

"Mr. Mayor," I said, "I have something to show you."

He walked over to me, and I took out the pail.

"What's this?" he said. "How nice."

"We have a problem," I said. "In our building . . ."

Was he listening to me? No. He was untying the string and lifting the lid right off the pail.

"Don't do that!" I said.

Too late. As soon as that rat saw daylight, it jumped out of the pail as fast as it could.

Well, you've never seen anything like what happened next. The mayor jumped three feet in the air. All the kids started screaming and climbing up on their chairs. The rat just ran.

Some of the mayor's assistants were yelling. Others were chasing the rat. When they cornered the rat, it turned around and chased them. I had to laugh—I couldn't help it.

Now, old Cheese-Breath wasn't stupid. The rat was looking for a way to get out of there. Finally it jumped up on the window ledge, squeezed through the wire mesh, and was gone.

After a few minutes everybody calmed down a little.

"Keesha!" Mrs. Perez said. "What in the world has gotten into you? Why did you play a silly joke like that?"

She was frowning at me, and so was the mayor and all his assistants. I could feel a lump in my throat, but I refused to cry.

"It wasn't a joke," I said. "I wanted the mayor to know how bad the rats are. They are the meanest, dirtiest, ugliest animals in the world. He must not know that, or why would he let them live all over our neighborhood?"

"Where did you get that rat?" the mayor asked.

"In my bedroom."

"You caught that thing in your bedroom?"

"Yes, sir. We just have too many rats."

"And you wanted to show me one so I would understand the problem?"

"That's right. I didn't mean for you to take the lid off the pail. I thought you could peek at the rat if you've never seen one."

"I've seen rats, but not that close." He looked at his assistants and chuckled.

I didn't see what was funny. "We see them that close all the time," I said.

"Okay," the mayor said, "you've made a strong point. And you're lucky, because the man to talk to, our commissioner of housing, is right here."

"I tried talking to him already," I said. I could tell the commissioner was getting a little nervous. "He didn't do a thing but waste my time and my mama's time."

The mayor looked at the commissioner, who shrugged and turned red.

The mayor said, "I'll make a deal with you, Keesha. Exterminators will be at your building by Friday morning. If they aren't, you can phone me directly. I'll tell my secretary to put your call right through. Is that fair?"

"That's fair," I said.

After the mayor left, Mrs. Perez said everything was okay, and that I had done the right thing. "Only . . . please, Keesha . . . no more rats in the classroom."

"I hope I never see a rat again, Mrs. Perez."

Then all the kids cheered for me.

But I'm waiting for Friday before I start cheering. If those exterminators don't show up, the mayor is going to get an earful, believe me.

Right now, I can't wait to get home and tell Mama everything that happened. She is going to be proud of me. I know it.

TEMPER, TEMPER

ADAPTED BY BRUCE LANSKY FROM AN
ITALIAN FOLKTALE

Italian Words:

Lira (pronounced "LEE-rah"): Italian money. One American
  dollar is worth about 1,500 lira.

Basta (pronounced "BA-stah"): means "enough."

Papa Giovanni was tired. Very tired. A drought the
previous summer had destroyed most of his crops,
leaving very little to eat, let alone sell. Yet somehow his
family had kept food on the table through the cold
winter. Papa Giovanni and his eldest son, Marco, had

worked odd jobs in town. His wife, Marcella, had awakened at five o'clock every morning to gather eggs and milk the cows. His second son, Nico, had delivered fresh milk and eggs to neighbors. His daughter, Francesca, had tutored children. Everyone had pitched in.

Now it was spring. But the rolling hills of Tuscany were not covered with lush green grass and budding trees. They were brown. Looking at the parched earth and sniffing the dusty air, Papa Giovanni made a decision.

That evening as the family ate a meager dinner of plain pasta, Papa Giovanni gazed sadly at their tired faces and said, "We don't have enough money to buy seeds. And even if we did, we don't even have enough water to grow weeds. I'm sorry to say that this farm can no longer support our family." He turned to Marco. "Marco, you are my oldest son. I must ask you to leave home and make your own way in the world. When you get a job, please send some money home until we get some rain. Good luck."

"I'll do my best, Papa," Marco replied dutifully.

The next morning Marco hugged his family goodbye and started off down the road with a spring in his step and hope in his heart. He was big and strong. He knew that his hardworking parents had done all they could for him. Now it was his turn to help them.

He walked until he came to a green valley. A stream rushed beside fields green with sprouting corn and wheat. Marco noticed a large farmhouse. A sign at the gate read "Help Wanted."

"This farm seems to be prosperous," thought Marco. "I'll try my luck here." He walked up the path to the front door and knocked.

It wasn't long before a beady-eyed farmer opened the door. "What do you want?" he asked.

"I'm looking for work," answered Marco. "Is the job still open?"

"Yes. Our field hand just quit. It isn't easy finding reliable help," the farmer replied grimly.

"You won't have to worry about me," said Marco. "I am as strong as an ox and won't quit until the job is done."

"You look strong enough," replied the farmer, "but you must prove you're not a quitter. If you leave before the crops are harvested, you won't get a single lira. If you stay, I'll give you ten million lira—more than most workers make in five years."

To Marco this job seemed almost too good to be

true. If he stayed on the job until harvest, he would make enough money to buy his family a new farm. "It's a deal!" he said.

Marco worked hard all summer weeding, watering, and fertilizing the crops and caring for the livestock. His room was comfortable, and he was given plenty of food and drink each day. He didn't see much of the farmer, but didn't think much of it. The only thing on Marco's mind was all the money he would receive after the crops were harvested.

But when harvest time came, things changed. Marco was served bread and water at breakfast, instead of ham and eggs. When Marco sat down in the field to eat lunch, the farmer rode up on a horse, cracked his whip, and shouted, "Get back to work, you sluggard. I should have known better than to hire you."

Marco was confused. "What are you talking about? I've worked hard all morning in the hot sun. I just stopped for lunch."

The farmer cracked his whip again, knocking Marco's bread out of his hand. "There's no time for lunch. Get back to work."

Burning with silent anger, Marco brushed the breadcrumbs from his pants, wiped his brow, and went back to picking corn.

That night no pasta and wine sat on Marco's dinner table—just a slice of bread and a glass of water. At four o'clock the next morning, a loud knocking at the door awakened Marco.

"Why are you still sleeping when you should be out in the field picking corn? If I'd known you were so lazy, I never would have hired you."

Marco grumbled as he dressed in the dark. No bread waited on the breakfast table—just a pitcher of water. He drank some and splashed the rest on his face to wake himself up. Then, tired and hungry, he walked slowly out to the fields.

Marco worked hard all morning. When the sun was directly overhead, he started walking back to the farmhouse for lunch. Up rode the farmer on his horse, cracking his whip in the air. "Get back to work, you weakling!" shouted the farmer.

Marco held his temper. "Don't worry; I'll go back to work as soon as I've had some lunch."

But the farmer kept goading him. "What kind of terrible parents would raise a good-for-nothing like you?"

"That does it!" flashed Marco. "When you insult my family, you go too far. I've put up with a lot of abuse, but I won't stand for it any longer. I quit!"

The farmer started to laugh. "I knew you were a quitter the moment I laid eyes on you. Since you've quit before the crops are harvested, you won't get paid. Pick up your belongings and get off my property."

Marco trudged homeward with the farmer's cruel laughter ringing in his ears. He kept thinking about all the money he would have earned if he had finished harvesting the crops. He had left home with hope in his heart, but now he had only tears in his eyes.

Papa Giovanni was looking out the window when Marco turned up the path. He noticed Marco's stooped shoulders and slow stride. He greeted his son with an embrace. Marco sobbed softly as he sank into his father's welcoming arms.

After supper the family crowded around Marco, and he told his sad story. Francesca was the first to comment. "You almost made it, Marco. Don't feel bad. That stingy crook took advantage of you. He worked you hard all summer, then tricked you into quitting."

"I'm proud of you," said Papa Giovanni. "You showed great restraint and only lost your temper when the farmer insulted your family. Now we know where ten million lira may be earned. Next year Nico can go back there and get it for us."

"I can't wait till spring, Papa," agreed Nico.

Papa Giovanni's family survived the winter as they had the previous year. By early spring, Nico was itching to get even with the cruel farmer.

As Nico set off down the road one morning, Marco yelled, "Remember, Nico, don't lose your temper—no matter what that buzzard says."

"Don't worry, Marco. I'll be back with the money this fall," Nico yelled back cheerfully.

Although Nico was not as big as his brother Marco, he was a very hard worker. Walking briskly down the road, Nico arrived at the stingy farmer's door before dark.

The farmer told Nico he needed a reliable worker who would not quit before the crops were harvested. He offered Nico ten million lira if he would work all summer, but no pay if he quit.

"It's a deal," said Nico with a smile. He knew what to expect. He would hold his temper no matter what.

Summer went smoothly for Nico, as it had for Marco. He worked hard, ate well, and was left alone. But when harvest time drew near, the cruel farmer began to harass Nico.

On the first harvest day, he rapped on Nico's door at four in the morning. "There's no time for breakfast today. So get going, you worthless mutt."

Nico grumbled, but controlled his temper. He knew that the war of nerves had begun.

The farmer said, "Don't bother coming in for lunch. I'll bring you something to eat." But when the sun was directly overhead, the farmer did not show up.

In fact, he didn't show up until five in the afternoon. He carried a bucket of dirty water. "Here's your lunch, you louse."

Nico stared at the cruel farmer but didn't say a word. He just kept working. The farmer went back to the farmhouse.

The next morning Nico awoke with a cold shock. The farmer had dumped a bucket of icy water on him. "You forgot your lunch," he sneered. "Today I want you to get an early start. I won't have you dawdling like that lazy bum who worked here last summer."

Still half asleep, Nico spoke without thinking. "How dare you talk about my brother that way? He was the best worker you ever had, you miserable miser."

The farmer just sneered, "You take after your lazy brother and your stupid parents."

Lying in bed drenched with cold water, Nico lost his temper. "That does it! You are more cruel and stingy than I ever thought possible. I quit!"

Realizing what he had said, Nico came to his senses. "I'm sorry I said that, sir. I lost my temper. Please, let me keep my job."

But the cruel farmer was laughing so loudly, he didn't hear Nico's apology. "I knew you were a quitter from the moment I met you. Now get off my property. And don't expect any pay for your work."

Nico got dressed in the dark and left, grieving because the stingy farmer had outsmarted him just as he had outsmarted Marco. On the long walk home, he kept thinking of how close he had come to earning ten million lira for his needy family.

That night, his sister Francesca comforted him. "Don't torture yourself, Nico. You almost pulled it off. Now, if I can learn from your experience, I think we'll have that ten million lira in our hands by next fall."

Papa Giovanni couldn't believe his ears. "Forget it, Francesca. Your brothers worked hard for two summers and didn't make a single lira. That farmer is a smart crook. Try your luck elsewhere."

"But Papa, I won't make the same mistakes my

brothers made. I'll figure out a new way to separate that crook from his cash." Francesca had made up her mind and no one could change it.

All winter she thought about how to outwit the farmer. When the first buds of spring appeared on the trees, she said good-bye to her family and walked down the road to seek her fortune.

"Remember to keep your temper," yelled Nico.

"Don't worry about me, Nico," Francesca called out, "I can handle that old buzzard."

When she saw a "Help Wanted" sign in front of a prosperous-looking farmhouse, she knew she had come to the right place. She was all smiles as the farmer told her how hard it was to find reliable workers. She said, "Don't worry about me; I won't quit. In fact, if I lose my temper, you don't have to pay me."

The stingy farmer could not believe his good fortune. Another goose had landed in his pond, and she was making it easy for him to pluck her feathers.

"Of course," continued Francesca, "if I stay until the crops are harvested, I'll expect a big reward."

"Agreed," said the farmer. "If you don't quit, I will pay you ten million lira."

"And if *you* lose your temper . . .," continued

Francesca.

"I won't lose my temper," snapped the farmer.

"But if you should," Francesca persisted, "then the money would be mine. Do you agree?"

"Of course," said the farmer. He showed her to her room and said, "I want to see you bright and early tomorrow. There is lots of work to do."

Francesca smiled. "Whatever you say, boss."

At daybreak the next morning, Francesca knocked on the farmer's bedroom door. "You said you wanted to see me bright and early. Well, here I am. What would you like me to do?"

The farmer cursed under his breath. "Clean out the stables," he barked, "And when you're done, mow and water the lawn."

"Whatever you say, boss," Francesca sang out as the farmer pulled the covers over his head.

Soon he was awakened again by a terrible noise. He jumped out of bed, pulled on his clothes, and ran out into the yard.

All the horses and cows were on the lawn just outside the farmer's bedroom window.

"What's the meaning of this?" he demanded.

"I did just what you said, boss. I cleaned all the

horses and cows out of the stables. They are now mowing and watering the lawn."

"That's not what I meant, you nincompoop!" he sputtered.

"Temper, temper," warned Francesca.

Remembering their agreement, the stingy farmer barked, "Go to the chicken coop and collect the eggs. Then feed the pigs."

"Whatever you say, boss," Francesca sang out as she picked up a basket and headed for the chicken coop.

Later the farmer dropped by the chicken coop and the pigpen to see how Francesca was doing. But he couldn't find her.

Then he heard a ruckus in the farmhouse. He couldn't believe his eyes when he looked into the dining room. Francesca had put plates on the floor for the pigs and was serving them savory omelets.

"What are you doing?" blustered the farmer.

"I'm doing exactly what you told me, boss. I gathered the eggs and now I'm feeding the pigs."

"You're crazy!" he shrieked.

"You'd better watch your fiery temper," she warned. "One day it will get you in trouble." Smiling, she continued to feed the pigs. The angry farmer stomped out of the dining room, afraid that he would lose all control.

Francesca soon followed him. "The pigs have finished their meal, boss. Now what do you want me to do?" she asked.

"Get those confounded pigs out of the dining room and sell them before I lose my temper," barked the angry farmer, trying to get rid of the nettlesome girl for a while.

"Whatever you say, boss," Francesca sang out as she headed for the dining room.

The farm was an hour from town by foot, so the farmer was surprised to see Francesca back in fifteen minutes without the pigs.

"Have you sold the pigs already?" he inquired.

"You told me to sell the pigs before you lost your temper. I figured you were going to lose your temper any minute, so I sold them as fast as I could," she explained.

"And what did get for them?"

"Well, on the road I met a man who asked me where I was going with the pigs. When I said I was taking them to market, he offered to buy them. 'How much will you pay?' I asked.

"'I have something worth far more than money,' he said.

"'What?' I asked.

"'Magic beans,' he answered. 'You may have heard of me. My name is Jack.'

"Well, of course I'd heard of Jack and his magic beans. You've heard of Jack, haven't you?"

"Enough of this nonsense," said the farmer. "How much money did he pay you for the pigs?"

"Money? He gave me five magic beans, which are worth a lot more than money. See? Here they are. Now I'll just plant them in your garden, and soon they'll grow as high as the sky."

"Magic beans! You sold my pigs for five beans?"

"Not only beans. Do you think I'm a fool? Your pigs are worth more than that."

The farmer, whose face had turned red with anger, breathed a sigh of relief. "How much did he pay you?"

"Well, he didn't exactly pay me any money. You see, in addition to the five beans, Jack also sang a song—"

"Wait a minute!" exploded the farmer. "Are you telling me that you sold my pigs to this fellow Jack for five magic beans and a song?"

"Yes, but it's not just any song. It's a special song

about pigs. Here's how it goes:

> *This little piggy went to market.*
> *This little piggy stayed home.*
> *This little piggy had roast beef.*
> *This little piggy had none.*
> *And this little piggy—"*

Francesca never did finish her song. The angry farmer screamed, "*Basta! Basta! Basta!* Enough already. You're driving me crazy. I want you to leave this farm and never come back again."

"I'm going to miss you and your fiery temper," Francesca said sweetly. "However, the ten million lira you promised me will ease my sorrow."

The farmer ran into his house and soon returned with the money. "Take the money, but leave at once!" he said bitterly.

"Thank you," she said politely. "In just a few days I have earned the money it took you years to accumulate by cheating my brothers and who knows how many others. When people hear about this, you won't be able to find any more free labor. You'll soon find out what it's like to do an honest day's work—and I don't think you'll like it. I think *you* are a quitter. And when you decide to quit farming, get in touch with me. Now I've got the money to buy this farm, and a hardworking family to make it prosper."

Francesca returned home with a smile on her face and joy in her heart. Her entire family met her at the gate, and they all burst into cheers when they saw how much money she had in her purse.

"Now we can start over!" shouted Marco and Nico.

"We can buy a new farm where the corn grows as high as a horse's ears; a farm with a deep well and plenty of water," said Papa Giovanni.

"I know of a beautiful farm that just might be for sale," said Francesca.

Skateboard Rosie and the Soda Kids

AN ORIGINAL STORY BY DIANE SAWYER

Spanish Words:

Hola (pronounced "O-la"): means "hi," "hello."

Amigos (pronounced "a-MEE-gos"): means "friends."

Skateboarding Terms:

Hang ten: all ten toes hang over the nose of the board.

Board-over-board: the skater jumps over another skateboard.

Frog stand: a handstand in which the skater's knees rest on her elbows.

Helicopter: a *hang ten* followed by a jump off the board and a complete 360-degree spin in the air.

Shoot the duck: the skater crouches and extends one leg forward.

Buddy-buddy: two skaters ride their boards holding hands.

Leg lift: standing on one foot, the skater extends the other leg straight up and holds it with one arm.

Kick turn: turning by weighting the tail of the board so the nose rises as the skater pivots on the rear wheels.

Bongo: to fall on the head.

Power slide: the skater crouches and makes a high-speed turn.

Rosie's shiny black ponytail whipped from side to side as she ran with her brother, Ray, across Cortez Street. On this bright Sunday morning in Tampa, Florida, palm trees rustled in the breeze.

Rosie gazed at the cotton-ball clouds hanging over the skyline. "No chance of rain to ruin our skate-boarding," she said. A lopsided grin lit up Ray's serious face.

Rosie hopped the curb and slung her helmet from her left arm. So did Ray. Waiting for the light to change at Alamanda Avenue, Rosie spun her skateboard wheels. Ray did too.

Rosie was glad Ray wasn't cooped up in his room with his baseball cards. But it was a real pain having an eight-year-old always hanging on her. Friday, after a bully had picked on Ray at the playground, Rosie had complained to her mother, "I can't always be there for him." Mrs. Sanchez had taken Rosie's chin in her strong hands and said, "Please, Rosie. Ray's small for a third-grader. He counts on you to protect him. And so do I."

Rosie and Ray trudged along for a half hour. They were headed for the parking lot of the abandoned soda factory, where they would skate.

"You'll like the factory," Rosie said encouragingly. "It's the best place to skate for miles around. The blacktop's in good shape and the loading ramps are great for jumps." When they turned the corner, the roar of skateboard wheels cracked the air.

"Who will be there today?" Ray asked.

"You never know," Rosie replied. "Kids from different schools have been hanging out and practicing there since the building burned down three years ago. We skate for competing teams, but we all get along." She smiled. "People call us the Soda Kids."

Ray pointed toward the factory parking lot. "They're skating in groups. And they look kinda tough. Are you sure they'll let us in?"

Rosie smiled. "Yeah. I skate with them all the time. But for now we'll stay out of their way."

"*Hola,* Rosie!" The Soda Kids shouted and waved.

"*Hola!*" Rosie hollered.

Carlos skated across the parking lot toward Rosie. His wiry body leaned purposefully over his board. He went to Southside Middle School and skated for their team, the Hurricanes. "We need an even number of skaters for our drills. Wanna join us?"

Rosie pouted. "I can't. I promised Ray I'd help him with his turns."

Ray looked at Carlos, his brown eyes pleading. "Can I skate with you and Rosie?"

"Listen, Peewee," Carlos said gruffly, "the first part of learning is watching. Stay put, and we'll show you the moves." Carlos spun around to Rosie. "Come on, girl. We're wasting time."

"Go ahead," Ray told Rosie. He plopped down on his skateboard.

Rosie dug her elbow pads and kneepads from her backpack and put on her gloves. Across the lot, she saw Lina, the captain of the Chargers, St. Mary's skateboard team, practicing power slides. Rosie's team, St. Anne's Speedettes, and the Chargers were Tampa's top two girls' teams, and they were fierce rivals.

Carlos whirled his arm over his head. "Let's show Rosie's baby bro our best stuff," he shouted.

The skaters charged. Juanita and Franco roared by, doing board-over-boards, with Juanita jumping over Franco's board as they skated. Little Zizi balanced on his board in a handstand, his elbows resting on his knees. "Nice frog, Zizi!" Rosie called. Jorge did a helicopter while Tommy shot the duck. Chi-Chi and Carmie dazzled Ray as they glided past in a buddy-buddy. Rosie finished off with leg lifts. Then everyone raced to the loading ramps and soared, spinning and twisting.

Suddenly Carlos, Jose, and Lina, the captains, raised their fists high over their heads and shook them twice. At this signal, Rosie and the other team members quickly lined up, left feet on their boards, right feet ready, itching to go. Another shake of their fists and Carlos, Jose, and Lina spun around and dropped their arms to their sides.

Little Zizi shouted, "Ready. Set. Go!"

"Charge!" "Go! Go!" "Faster!" The captains' commands boomed over the roaring wheels. They led their teammates in a challenging zigzag course around piles of tin cans. Then, crouching, the twelve kids zoomed past Ray in straight downhill runs, their ponytails, pigtails, and rattails flying out behind them. Carlos's team, with Rosie in second position, reached the fence first. Victory cheers pierced the air.

Ray jumped up, cheering, proud of his Rosie and amazed by the Soda Kids. He'd heard about them from Rosie and recognized several of them from school, but he'd never seen them skate. Until today, Mama had only let him practice on the sidewalk in front of their house.

Carlos and Rosie spun toward Ray, flipped their boards, and caught them. Carlos bent close to Ray. "Hey, Peewee, you ready?"

Rosie remembered Mama's words: "Stick close to Ray." She ruffled her brother's curly black hair. "I promised Ray I'd show him kick turns and hang tens."

Carlos squinted at Rosie. "How come you're not practicing with the Speedettes?"

"We're getting together this afternoon." Rosie rolled her eyes toward Ray. "When my mother finishes her shift at the nursing home."

Lina wheelied to a stop between Rosie and Carlos. "Hey, Runt." She shoved a tissue under Ray's nose. "Practice wiping away your tears. Your sister's going to lose the relay race to me."

Rosie pushed Lina's hand away. "Save that for your own crying session," she snapped.

"Hey, Rosie girl." Carlos nudged Rosie with his elbow and winked. "Don't fight with Lina, unless it's over me."

Rosie backed away, annoyed.

"Yuck! Pink." Lina curled her lip and pointed at the pink lightning bolt Rosie had laminated onto her board. "Pink for the Speedettes."

Rosie's face lit up. "Yeah. We're fast as lightning. The best twelve-year-old-division girls' relay team in Tampa."

Lina plunked her hands on her hips. "Don't count on first prize. My Chargers have that all sewed up."

Rosie's dark eyes glistened defiantly. She imagined the cheers as the Speedettes, dressed in pink satin shirts and shorts, zoomed toward the judges' table. She pictured Lina and the Chargers in their zebra-striped outfits, hanging their heads, resigned to second place.

"Pink." Lina sniffed. "That fits you baby girls." She skated away, sneering at Rosie over her shoulder. Carlos chased after her.

"Teach me stuff," Ray said, tugging at Rosie's T-shirt.

Rosie yanked up Ray's droopy shorts. She wasn't cut out to be an older sister. Impatiently, she barked commands at Ray: "Push off. Pump your arms. Crouch. Stop. Don't bongo." She picked him up over and over. "This is a waste of time," she told herself. "Mama is not being fair. I'm losing my friends because of Ray."

Rosie kept showing Ray how to balance himself. Finally he got on the board and rolled down the incline, waving to Rosie, proud of his accomplishment. Rosie saw Lina practicing jumps with Carlos. "We'll work on safety now," she lectured, exasperated. "Remember how we practiced falling at home?"

Ray nodded. "Squat down, stay loose, protect my head and spine. I'm not a baby, Rosie. I can remember what you tell me."

As the sun rose higher, Ray mastered the basic moves and safety techniques. Finally he managed to skate faster than he could run, but he was still a klutz on turns.

It was only a little after eleven when Rosie told Ray, "We'd better go home for lunch now." She felt guilty dragging him away so early. But if they hurried, she could fix lunch, dump Ray as soon as Mama got home, and meet the Speedettes by one o'clock. She didn't want to let her team down.

Rosie and Ray waved good-bye to the Soda Kids

and began the long trek home.

"Carlos and Hector live here on Factory Street," Rosie said as they passed by sandlot lawns and cement-block houses with peeling paint. Yucca plants with stiff, spearlike leaves stood guard at the windows. Scraggly palm trees lined the streets and alleys, shading the garbage cans at the curbs.

Rosie wished they could skateboard instead of walking, but she had promised her mother they wouldn't skate on the streets. They had walked only two blocks when Ray began to dawdle. He was hot and tired from skateboarding.

"We'll cut up the alley behind the boarded-up strip mall," Rosie said, trying to speed him up. "The alley's paved. We can skate the whole thing."

"Mama said not to skate on the street."

"But it's an alley, not a street." She nudged him along.

"There are too many dogs here," Ray objected.

"Don't be such a scaredy cat," Rosie said. "How can the dogs hurt us when they're locked behind wooden fences? They can't even see us."

"Sure is a lot of barking," Ray said. He hung back. "Do you think Mr. Fuego's pit bulls are in his yard?" He pointed to the house where Mr. Fuego, their plumber, lived. Mr. Fuego was always boasting about his watchdogs.

Suddenly the dogs appeared at the top of the fence, their mouths foaming, their jagged teeth glistening, their eyes filled with fury.

Ray gasped. "It's Bent-Ear and Scar-Face." He moved away from the fence, and scooted past several palm trees.

Keeping her eyes riveted on the fence, Rosie hurried after Ray to the mall side of the alley. An icy shiver crept up her back.

Ray squinted his eyes and looked up at Rosie. "I don't like Bent-Ear and Scar-Face," he said. "They scare me." Ray stopped suddenly and grabbed Rosie by the arm. "Rosie, look," he said, his voice rising in terror. "The latch is off Mr. Fuego's gate."

"We have to get out of here," Rosie whispered.

"I'm scared." Ray's voice trembled.

"Put on your helmet. Fast," Rosie insisted.

Rosie helped Ray buckle his helmet. They jumped on their skateboards. They pushed hard, but the rough pavement caught at their wheels. They pumped frantically with their arms.

Rosie glanced back at Mr. Fuego's gate. Bent-Ear

and Scar-Face had broken out. "Hurry, Ray. They're after us," she shouted. The dogs came closer and closer. They leaped up and threw their full weight on Ray. His skateboard flew, ricocheted off the wall, and rolled toward the fence. Ray sprawled on the ground.

Rosie wheelied to a stop. The dogs turned on her. They charged and knocked her down. Though dizzy and frightened, she could think only of Ray, helpless. He needed her. Now the dogs were sniffing his limp body. She grabbed her skateboard and held it in front of her like a shield. She pushed herself up, her back braced by the fence.

"Down! Down, boys!" she yelled. The dogs turned back toward her, growled, and bared their teeth. They approached slowly, panting in her face, pinning her to the fence. Rosie saw Ray across from her in the alley, crawling.

"Run for it," Rosie shouted, relieved that he could move.

Ray covered his eyes and began to scream. The dogs snarled and yelped. Charging over to Ray, they clawed at the pavement by his feet. Their noses poked at his legs, arms, and back.

"Help me, Rosie," Ray screamed. Rosie picked up

her skateboard and swung it with all her might. The dogs backed off, bared their teeth, pulled their heads down low, and circled Ray. Low rumbling noises came from deep in their throats.

"Get up, Ray," Rosie yelled, swinging the skateboard again. "Come on, get up," she screamed. But Ray froze, terrified. The dogs circled him, growling.

Rosie stood up, spun her skateboard wheels, and banged her fist on the fence behind her. The dogs turned toward the noise. Saliva dripped from their mouths.

Rosie shouted at the dogs, "Come and get me, you big bullies. Leave my brother alone." The dogs glared and snorted, pacing between her and Ray.

Rosie noticed that the dogs ran toward whoever moved quickly and made noise. "Ray, listen to me," Rosie said. Her voice shook, and her legs wobbled. "I'll make the dogs chase your skateboard. Then I'll lock you in Mr. Fuego's yard and go for help."

"Okay," Ray whimpered.

Rosie picked up Ray's skateboard and spun the wheels. She banged it against the fence and garbage cans. She flung her arms and legs every which way. "Yee-ha! Yee-ha!" she whooped, then hurled the skateboard down the alley. The dogs charged after it.

"Come on, Ray!" Grabbing her skateboard and Ray's hand, Rosie raced into Mr. Fuego's yard. "Stay here," she ordered. "The dogs can't get in. I'm going for help. There's a pay phone on the next street."

Ray nodded. Tears streamed down his cheeks. "Hurry, Rosie."

Rosie quickly locked the gate. She jumped on her skateboard and shot down the alley. She heard the dogs bounding after her, their nails scratching the stony pavement. Choking back tears, she shouted for help as she raced along, gliding and pushing, faster and faster, but no one came to her rescue. "Skate to the phone and dial 911," she told herself. "Hurry."

She leaned over her board and zoomed onward, thinking of Ray. Mama would never forgive her if anything happened to him. And Rosie would never forgive herself.

Rosie slam-stopped between two parked cars. Holding her skateboard under one arm, she carefully crossed the street. She waved her free arm, hoping someone would stop, but no one did. Leaping back onto her skateboard, she sped down the deserted sidewalk. Scar-Face and Bent-Ear had not followed her across the street. Instead, they turned around and ran back toward their yard, where Ray was waiting.

Rosie stopped at the pay phone. It had been ripped from the box. She nearly sobbed. She glanced up and down the street. No police cars. Her heart pounded. She gulped shards of air.

She was Ray's only hope. He was safe for now, but the fence was rickety and the dogs were angry. She pictured Ray sobbing alone in the yard, and the dogs, the enemy, trying to break in. Wait! Enemy! Of course! Dogs had enemies too.

Rosie knew exactly what she had to do.

Mustering her strength, Rosie raced the three blocks to the soda factory. "Hey, Carlos!" she shouted. She didn't call out, "Help! Some pit bulls are going to attack Ray." She didn't want the Soda Kids to see Ray hiding behind a fence, crying his eyes out. He'd never live it down.

"And that rotten Lina," Rosie thought. "She'd spread the word that my brother's a crybaby. Every skateboarder in Tampa would be laughing at him."

Carlos whipped across the parking lot toward Rosie, with Hector at his heels. They came to a sharp stop in front of her, kicking their boards up and catching them. "What's up?" Carlos asked.

"Carlos, you live on the same block as Mr. Fuego, right?" Rosie asked. Carlos nodded. "I need your cat, Diablo, right away. Ray's trapped in Mr. Fuego's yard, and Fuego's pit bulls are in the alley. I can't get Ray out alone. I need Diablo's help."

Carlos grinned. "Girl, my Diablo is gonna love taking on Scar-Face and Bent-Ear. Those dogs have been hassling him for years. It's payback time." Carlos stuck out his chest. "Let's find out, once and for all, who owns that alley."

"Hey, Rosie," Hector said, "I live next to Carlos, and my cat, Fireball, is bigger and meaner than Diablo. Give him a chance, too."

"Okay," Rosie said, "Fireball's in. But don't tell the other kids what we're up to." She checked her watch. Ray had been alone almost ten minutes. "We better hurry."

"Leave it to me," Carlos said. He zoomed off, spoke to Chi-Chi and Lina, and raced back. "I told them we're gonna pick up some food. They'll wait right here."

Rosie urged, "Come on. Let's go get your cats!"

Carlos and Hector jumped onto their skateboards, shot through the opening in the fence, hit the sidewalk, and flew onto the street, following Rosie's lead. They caught up and roared past on either side of her, heading straight for their yards.

Carlos quickly returned with Diablo, a huge, growling, spitting, jabbing ball of black fur, in his arms. Hector reappeared, clutching Fireball to his chest.

Fireball shrieked. His orange-red fur was standing on end. Diablo yowled back.

The scruffy cats had never looked so good to Rosie. Tears spilled onto her cheeks. "Hurry!" she shouted.

The kids swooped down the sloping street. Forward, forward, faster and faster they skated, rocketing along. They crouched tight, veered left, skating with dizzying speed, and blasted into the alley. Carlos and Hector lifted Diablo and Fireball shoulder high. The cats flattened their ears and clawed the air. They drew back their lips and hissed. Their tails whipped around wildly.

The deafening roar of wheels bounced off the buildings in the alley. Bent-Ear and Scar-Face stopped pawing Mr. Fuego's fence to stare at the advancing skateboarders and cats. Rosie shouted, "We're coming, Ray. Hold on!"

Rosie, Carlos, and Hector bore down on the dogs.

Diablo and Fireball went wild, wailing and shrieking, their paws jabbing. They leaped free and dove toward the garbage cans. Howling and yowling, Bent-Ear and Scar-Face chased the cats and crashed into the cans. Lids clattered. Papers and vegetable peelings flew. Bottles and cans rolled.

Dodging the debris, Fireball sunk his claws into a palm tree and flew up the trunk. Screeching, Diablo raced up the next palm tree. The cats glared down from their perches, hissing and screeching, wild-eyed. The dogs paced back and forth between the trees, barking and growling, their fury turning into frustration.

Rosie eased over to the fence. She heard Ray sobbing. "It's safe to come out," she whispered, unlatching the gate. "The dogs have forgotten us."

Ray stumbled from the yard. Rosie hugged him, then looked over her shoulder to make sure the cats and dogs were still at a standoff. "Let's go," she said, hurrying Ray along in case the dogs changed their minds.

"Come on, little bro," Carlos said, cuffing Ray's chin gently with his knuckles.

When they had turned the corner, Rosie stopped and hugged Ray again. "Let me see what the dogs did to you. Are you okay?" She breathed easier when she saw that his scratches were superficial. "I should never have taken that shortcut."

"I'm okay," Ray said, brushing her hands aside.

Carlos tousled Ray's hair. "You hung tough, Peewee."

Ray kicked the sidewalk. "Yeah," he said, then looked up worriedly. "Will the cats be okay?"

Carlos grinned. "They'll be home before you can call the Animal Control Center. Diablo's one tough dude."

"Come on, man," Hector said. "Fireball's tougher."

Carlos spun his wheels at Ray. "We gotta go. My stomach's growling for some chips and salsa. See you around, *amigos*!"

Rosie held her board aloft like a banner and spun the wheels in salute. "Thanks for helping me with my brother." She grinned. "Tell Lina that she and the Chargers better gear up for next week's relay race. I've just improved my speed."

SAVE WELLINGTON WOODS!!

An Original Story by Laurie Eynon

No one was more upset than Emily when Ms. Hopper told her science class that Wellington Woods was going to be bulldozed to build houses.

"What?" exclaimed Emily, leaping to her feet and knocking her *Peterson's Guide to Birds of Eastern Canada* on the floor.

"Settle down, Emily," chided Ms. Hopper. "I know it's disappointing." She turned her back to the class and stared out the window at a large green area of trees that began at the far edge of the schoolyard. Because the area was so near Wellington Middle School, it had always been known as Wellington Woods, even though the school did not own it. The woods were one of very few patches of green left in the growing Toronto suburb, not far from Lake Ontario. Trees, bushes, flowers, and grass were being replaced with residential buildings, parking lots, and malls.

"How will we do our leaf collections?" asked Andy Chu.

"And bird identification?" someone else asked.

"We won't have such a convenient place for nature study anymore," Ms. Hopper said. "We'll have to identify plants and birds by looking at pictures. The pond where we collect algae to study under the microscope will be drained. The saplings we planted last spring will be uprooted." She shook her head sadly.

Emily's spirit sank. Science class would never be the same without Wellington Woods. And science class was Emily's favorite—especially the study of plants and animals. She dreamed of being a naturalist someday. She pictured herself in a khaki uniform and sturdy hiking boots, leading tourists through Banff National Park.

"Where will the animals go?" asked Sheryl Sanders.

Emily knew Sheryl was thinking about the baby bunnies she'd stumbled over during one of their walks last spring.

"I just don't know," mumbled Ms. Hopper.

Neither did Emily. Everything near the Wellington school was filled with shopping malls, houses, or factories.

Emily walked home from school to the small, sunny apartment where she lived with her mother.

"Hey, watch it," warned her mother, who was putting away groceries. "Get those muddy shoes off and put them on that newspaper. Honestly, Em, do you purposely step into mudholes?"

"The trillium is starting to bloom," replied Emily. "I had to walk through some mud to look at it up close."

"Checking out wildflowers again?" asked her mom.

"Yup," replied Emily glumly.

"Judging by your long face, I guess you've heard the news," said her mom as she set a box of granola on the shelf. "I heard that your woods are going to be cleared to make way for a new housing development."

"It's not 'my woods,' Mom," said Emily. "If it were, it wouldn't be torn down. There are other places to build houses. Why build them on the only woods in our part of town?"

"For money, of course," said her mother. "People will pay a lot to live so close to schools and shopping."

"There are more important things than money," Emily shot back.

Her mother laughed. "You don't have to tell me, Emily. I agree with you! But then, we've never had much money, so what do we know?"

"We know that cutting down the woods is wrong," said Emily.

"Well, Jack Dubois owns the property," said her mother. "He can do what he wants with it."

Everyone knew Jack Dubois, the real-estate tycoon. He had built the Dubois Office Towers downtown as well as numerous apartment buildings and shopping centers. Emily had often seen his picture in the newspapers and on TV.

"It's too bad, Emily," continued her mom. "But cheer up. You'll be a naturalist someday, with or without Wellington Woods."

The next day Ms. Hopper took the class for a walk through Wellington Woods. "One last time," she said. "The bulldozers will be here on Monday."

"Can't we do something?" said Sheryl Sanders.

"I don't know what," said Ms. Hopper. "The land belongs to Mr. Dubois. Perhaps we should be glad he's left it alone as long as he has."

"Does he know how much we use Wellington Woods?" asked Emily.

Ms. Hopper sighed. "Several people, including me, phoned Mr. Dubois. But his office always says he's busy. He's avoiding us."

For the rest of the day, Emily couldn't concentrate on her schoolwork.

"Earth to Emily," Mr. Chester said during history class. "Hello, is there any intelligent life in there?"

Emily's face flushed as the other kids laughed.

"We're talking about the sixties," said Mr. Chester. "Love-ins, flower children, and bell-bottoms. Did you read the chapter?"

Emily hadn't, but she piped right up. "I know a lot about the sixties," she said. "My mother was a flower child in New York City. I saw a picture of her in our album wearing love beads and long hair. Her family came to Canada in the sixties to protest the Vietnam War. She was also a freedom rider."

"That's very interesting, Emily," said Mr. Chester. "Many Americans immigrated to Canada to protest that war. But tell us what a freedom rider is."

"My mom," said Emily proudly, "went to Columbia University. She rode a bus to Alabama with a bunch of other Columbia University students to protest segregation. You know, like making black people and white people go to separate schools." Emily looked around at the faces of her friends—black, Asian, Indian. She was glad her school had all kinds of students.

"That's right, Emily," said Mr. Chester. "Your mother was part of an important era." He paused. "But you still ought to read the chapter."

Emily sighed. "Yes, Mr. Chester."

Emily pictured her mom in her college days, carrying signs and shouting slogans. Her present-day mom was far from a rebel. She worked in a bookstore, ate health food, and wore sensible shoes. When she talked about her radical youth, she'd say, "It was another time. I believed I could change the world. Now I know you can't make the world be exactly how you want it. But," she always added, "that doesn't mean you shouldn't keep trying."

Emily pictured herself as a radical—storming into Mr. Dubois's office and demanding that Wellington Woods be saved. But she knew she'd get laughed at. Or thrown out. Or both. One girl couldn't stop a powerful man like Jack Dubois. And she sure as heck couldn't stop a bulldozer.

Mr. Chester was still talking. "The sixties were a time of great idealism among young people. They believed they could change the world for the better. And many of the changes people struggled for back then— like school integration—did come about."

Emily listened. Changes *had* happened, but not easily. Sometimes it must have seemed hopeless, yet they didn't give up. "And I can't give up either," she thought. "Anyway, I'm not trying to change the whole world. Just one little part of it in Ontario called Wellington Woods." She knew what she had to do.

After school, Emily stopped kids as they came out the doors and told them her idea. "Spread the word," she said.

All weekend, she called more students and asked them to call others. She went over to Sheryl Sanders's house on Sunday afternoon with colorful markers and a stack of poster board.

On Monday morning Ms. Hopper arrived at school a little late. She rushed into her room to find it nearly empty. She looked out the window for some sign of the missing students. "They can't all be sick!" she said. Then she looked toward Wellington Woods.

She grabbed her sweater and headed out the door with several other teachers close behind her. "What's happening?" they asked. "Where are all the kids?"

The first one they saw was Sheryl Sanders. She was sitting on a low tree branch, holding a big sign that read, "WHERE WILL THE ANIMALS GO?" Then they saw Andy Chu standing in the pond with his jeans rolled up to his knees. He was holding a sign that read, "THIS IS OUR SCIENCE CLASSROOM!" Dozens of kids circled the trees, perched on rocks, sat along the edge of the pond—they were all over Wellington Woods.

When the sound of bulldozers drew near, Emily raised the bullhorn one of the cheerleaders had loaned her. "We, the students of Wellington School, protest the destruction of this land," she shouted. "Save Wellington Woods!"

The rest of the students chimed in, "Save Wellington Woods!"

The bulldozers stopped at the edge of the woods.

"Hey, teach, get these kids outta here," one of the workers said to Ms. Hopper.

Ms. Hopper responded by planting herself beside

Emily, folding her arms, and joining the chant: "Save Wellington Woods!"

Within minutes, newspaper and TV reporters arrived. Andy Chu had made some anonymous calls that tipped them off to the protest.

"We want to talk to Jack Dubois," Emily told the reporters. "He should know that Wellington Woods is our nature laboratory, not just some trees and a pond."

"That's right," said Ms. Hopper. "The students learn more from these woods than they could ever learn from a textbook."

"Our city will be nothing but concrete and steel if Wellington Woods is destroyed," Emily pleaded. She had prepared what she would say. "Plants will die. Animals will be homeless. Trees keep our air clean—they are the lungs of the earth! Birds traveling south use the pond as a stopover. Species loss is a major problem that—"

"Break it up, folks!" shouted a policeman who had just arrived. A few other squad cars soon pulled up. Emily swallowed hard and kept right on talking.

"Destroying these woods is wrong!" she shouted.

"Save Wellington Woods!" The cry went up again.

The police took their time rounding up the students and getting them back to class. The bulldozers had already gone.

"But they'll be back bright and early tomorrow," sighed Ms. Hopper. "We've only gained a temporary reprieve."

Emily was still shouting "Save Wellington Woods!" into the bullhorn when a policeman escorted her out of the woods. He said quietly, "My boy loved these woods when he went to school here, too."

The evening news was full of stories and pictures of the "Save Wellington Woods" effort. A closeup of Emily shouting into the bullhorn flashed across the TV screen. Emily's mother was shocked.

"Emily!" she exclaimed.

"I had to do what I thought was right, Mom," said Emily. "Like you did in the sixties."

"Oh, Emily." Her mother hugged her. "The environment is a noble cause. I just hope you won't be too disappointed."

"Mom, I'd only be disappointed in myself if I didn't try to do something," said Emily. "Years ago black people couldn't go to the same schools as whites. You protested that. And it changed! Look at my own school."

"I guess that's true," agreed her mother. "But there

are still so many problems!"

"Yes," said Emily. "And that's why we have to keep trying—like I'm trying to help save the woods."

Emily's mom smiled. "I'm proud of you," she said. "No matter what Jack Dubois decides."

Early Tuesday morning, the bulldozers weren't there yet, but something was going on. Emily, Ms. Hopper, and all the kids hurried over.

In front of Wellington Woods, two workers were erecting a sign. It read:

DUBOIS WOODS AND NATURE PRESERVE
Dedicated to the students of Wellington School
by the generosity of Mr. Jack H. Dubois

Soon the TV and newspaper people arrived. Then a black limousine pulled up. A dapper, silver-haired man in a dark blue suit got out, straightened his tie, stood next to the sign, and smiled broadly for the cameras.

"People of the city," he said as the cameras flashed, "and students of Wellington School . . . I, Jack Dubois, have decided to keep this little nature preserve just as it is for the students of Wellington School to use. I will do my part to preserve the environment."

A big cheer went up from the crowd.

"I can't believe it!" exclaimed Ms. Hopper.

"Maybe we misjudged Mr. Dubois," said Emily. "He's a nature lover after all."

But Mr. Dubois was not finished talking. "I also want to take this opportunity," he said, "to announce that I am running for parliament in the next election. I will, if elected, listen to all our citizens and fight for their concerns."

Ms. Hopper laughed. "Some nature lover," she said to Emily. "Dubois knows the negative publicity he'd get if he tore down the woods would damage his campaign. He'd appear antienvironment and antieducation. This protest you kids arranged is just the kind of publicity he doesn't need. His image is more important to him than his bankroll right now."

"So you mean," said Emily, "that he did the right thing, but for the wrong reason?"

Ms. Hopper laughed again. "That's right, Emily."

"I can live with that," Emily said with a smile.

"Dubois Woods. I guess we'll have to get used to calling it that," said Ms. Hopper.

But everyone called it Wellington Woods anyway.

THE APPLE PIE HOUSE

AN ORIGINAL STORY BY JANET SMITH

Spanish Words:

Buenos dias (pronounced "BWAY-nos DEE-ahs"): means "good day" or "good morning."

Señora (pronounced "sen-YO-rah"): means "Mrs."

Manzana (pronounced "mahn-ZAH-nah"): means "apple."

Burros (pronounced "BOO-rros"): means "donkeys."

Bolivares (pronounced "boh-lee-vah-res"): Venezuelan money. One American dollar is equal to about 470 bolivares.

Gracias (pronounced "GRAH-see-ahs"): means "thank you."

Ms. Walker sat in her tin-roofed mud-block house in Acarigua, Venezuela—a long way from her home in

Deer River, Minnesota. She had come here to teach English, and a teacher from Acarigua had gone to Deer River to teach Spanish.

Ms. Walker's books were open in front of her. It was Saturday, and she was preparing her lessons for the next week. She glanced at her watch. It was almost nine o'clock, and Maria wasn't there yet. That wasn't like Maria. Twelve-year-old Maria was Ms. Walker's best pupil.

Soon after Ms. Walker came to Acarigua, she'd decided that she needed someone to help her in her little house. She asked Maria to recommend someone, and Maria had said that she would like the job herself. Since then, the two of them were together more than they were apart. Ms. Walker had grown very fond of Maria.

Maria walked slowly to Mrs. Walker's house. She loved working for the lady from the faraway place. She had learned much from her, both in school and while helping her at home. Maria thought about the part of her job she liked best—baking in the funny little tin box that sat on Ms. Walker's gas stove. Ms. Walker had taught her to read many English words from a well-used *Betty Crocker Cookbook.*

Maria unlatched the gate in front of Ms. Walker's

house. Usually, she called out a cheery *"Buenos dias, Señora* Walker" when she arrived, but today was different. Today she didn't feel like greeting anyone or smiling. She felt more like crying.

Ms. Walker heard Maria come in through the back door, and she went to see what she was doing. She found Maria sitting at the kitchen table, paging through the cookbook.

"Do you feel like baking today?" Ms. Walker asked.

"Yes," Maria said sadly. "But it must be something very special."

"Are you celebrating something?" Ms. Walker asked.

"No," Maria answered. "This might be the worst day that ever was."

"Tell me what is bothering you," Ms. Walker said. "Maybe together we can figure out what to do about it." Ms. Walker pulled out a chair and sat at the little wooden table across from Maria.

"I don't think there is anything we can do," Maria said. "My family is going to lose our house."

Ms. Walker pictured Maria's house. Like most of the houses in Acarigua, it wasn't fancy. Mud bricks had been baked in the hot tropical sun and set in a wooden framework. Wet mud splashed between the bricks held the house together. It wasn't much, but it was Marie's home.

"Why are you going to lose your house?" Ms. Walker asked.

"A man from the government gave a paper to everyone on our street," Maria explained. "He said the government is going to tear down all our houses to make room for a health clinic."

Maria reached into her skirt pocket, took out the letter, and handed it to Ms. Walker. Ms. Walker read it carefully, making sure she understood all the Spanish words. There was no doubt about it: Maria's house would soon be nothing but a memory.

"It's good that Acarigua will have a new clinic," Ms. Walker said thoughtfully, "but it's very sad that your house will be torn down. Isn't there something we can do?"

"The paper says that the government will give us a little piece of land in another place," said Maria. "But what good is a piece of land? We don't have enough money to build a house on it. It won't be so bad during the dry season, but when the rains start. . . ."

Ms. Walker nodded. Acarigua was right in the middle of the Venezuelan plains. The rains lasted more than four months. It rained so hard, one couldn't even cross the street. The houses all had holes in the floor along their walls so that when the rains stopped, people could push the water outside with a rubber squeegee. No, there was no way to live outside in Acarigua during the rainy season.

Ms. Walker gave the letter back to Maria and asked, "Do you think you might feel better if you bake something?"

Maria smiled back at her. "I always feel better when I am baking," she answered.

Maria studied the recipes for a long time. She understood some of the words, but others looked funny. Finally, she asked, "*Señora* Walker, what is ah-play pee-ay?"

"Ah-play pee-ay?" Ms. Walker asked. "I don't know. Show me."

Maria turned the cookbook toward Ms. Walker and pointed to a recipe for apple pie.

"That is apple pie," Ms. Walker told Maria, saying the words slowly. She explained that apple pie and baseball were very popular in the United States.

"Apple pie," Maria said, copying Ms. Walker's pronunciation. She looked at the recipe again. "It looks like ah-play pee-ay to me."

"Then ah-play pee-ay it is," Ms. Walker said, laughing. "Do you want to make some?"

"I don't know," Maria said. "What is an ah-play?"

"An ah-play—or apple—is a *manzana,*" Ms. Walker explained. She reached toward the kitchen shelf where she kept her cookbook and a few other things she had brought from Minnesota. She picked up a small crystal apple flecked with gold. "Like this," Ms. Walker said. "Of course, real apples are red, green, or yellow. This one was a present from my grandmother. I used to climb the apple tree in her backyard. She gave this to me on my tenth birthday and said I would never have to steal her apples again, because now I had one of my own."

Maria laughed. "Your grandmother must have been funny," she said. "Yes, I have seen those . . . apples . . . at the open market."

Ms. Walker loved to go to the open market. It was a place in the center of Acarigua where people sold all sorts of things: food, pottery, blankets, clothes, games. People came from many miles away to buy and sell things at the market.

"We don't have ah-plays in Acarigua," Maria said. "They don't grow in such hot places."

"We can make something else," Ms. Walker said, turning pages in the cookbook.

"No," Maria insisted. "We will find some ah-plays. I've seen them often at the market. They bring them down from the mountains on *burros*. I will go and buy some; then I will be back."

Maria seemed much happier as she skipped to the door. She was gone less than a minute before she poked her head back into the house.

"*Señora,*" she said, "may I have my wages for the next week?"

"Or course," Ms. Walker said. She was glad to see Maria in a better mood. She carefully counted out twenty bolivares and handed them to Maria.

"But I will have to work for a long time to earn this much money!" Maria exclaimed.

"We will call it your birthday present—early." Ms. Walker smiled at Maria.

"Oh, *gracias, Señora!*" Maria said, once again skipping out the door. "I'll be back soon."

Ms. Walker tried to resume her lesson planning, but she couldn't keep her mind on her work. She kept looking at her watch every few minutes. Maria was taking an awfully long time to buy a few apples.

Finally Ms. Walker heard something outside and looked out the window. She saw Maria holding a brown paper bag under one arm and pulling her sister's little red wagon with the other hand. The wagon was loaded with burlap bags full of apples.

"What are you going to do with all those apples?" Ms. Walker asked, holding the door open as Maria pulled the wagon into the house.

"I am going to make ah-play pee-ay," Maria answered. She put down the paper bag. "You will help me, no?"

"Of course I will help you," Ms. Walker answered, "but you need only a few apples to make a pie. You have bought every apple in Acarigua!"

"I did." Maria grinned. "I went to every shop in the whole town. Not one apple is left. I need all the ah-play pee-ays I can make." She pointed to the brown paper bag on the floor. "I also bought some pie pans and paper towels. You don't have enough for the number of pies I want to bake."

Ms. Walker wondered why Maria needed paper towels. Maybe for cleaning up afterward. "Why do you need so many pies?" she asked.

"Because it takes a lot of ah-play pee-ay to build a house!"

Ms. Walker looked at Maria and shook her head. Surely Maria knew she couldn't make a house out of apple pies. But Maria reassured Ms. Walker that she knew what she was doing.

Maria and Ms. Walker began peeling the apples. The long red peels curled and dropped onto a big pile. "Maybe someday ah-play pee-ay will be as popular in Venezuela as in America," Maria joked.

When they had peeled and sliced all the apples, Ms. Walker explained how to mix them with flour, sugar, and cinnamon. Maria looked in the cupboards for a bowl big enough to hold all the apples. She couldn't find one, so she washed out the wagon, put a big clean towel in it, and dumped in the apples. Then she stirred the flour, sugar, and cinnamon in a big pan and poured the mixture over the apples. Ms. Walker watched as Maria mixed it all together with her hands.

"There," Maria said, brushing her sticky hands. "Now all I have to do is make the crust, right?"

"Yes," Ms. Walker said. She had already taught Maria how to make pie crust, but with so many pies to make, she offered to help.

"No," Maria refused. "I want to do the rest myself. I want the ah-play pee-ay house to be all mine."

Ms. Walker shook her head again. There was no point arguing with Maria. She had made up her mind, so Ms. Walker decided to let her try making a house out of the pies. But what would she say when Maria stacked the pies and they all fell down? This was silly behavior from a girl who was usually so sensible.

Ms. Walker went into the living room and worked on her lessons, leaving Maria alone with her apple pies. She turned her electric fan on high. The temperature inside the house was climbing by the minute with the stove running continuously.

Maria worked all afternoon. It was almost five o'clock when Maria announced, "The ah-play pee-ays are all done!"

"What are you going to do with them now?" asked Ms. Walker.

"Why don't you come with me and find out?" Maria invited. Ms. Walker quickly agreed. She was too curious to stay at home.

Maria carefully set a row of three apple pies in the little red wagon. Then she set six sticks carefully in place—one in each corner and one in the middle of each long side. She took a board and set it—oh so gently—on top of the sticks. Then she set another row of apple pies on the board. Ms. Walker watched, holding her breath for fear the pies would fall down, as Maria tied a rope around the sticks to hold them in place. She repeated this until she had six rows of apple pies—eighteen pies in all—loaded onto the wagon. Maria then tucked a roll of paper towels and a knife into the wagon.

Ms. Walker held the door open for Maria and the wagon, then followed her down the street. Maria walked very slowly. She walked past her house. She walked past her friends, who all asked her, "Maria, what is that?"

"It is ah-play pee-ay," Maria answered. "It is as American as baseball!"

"It smells good," one woman said. "What are you going to do with it?"

"Would you like to buy some?" Maria asked.

"Yes," the woman said, licking her lips at the thought of tasting such a treat. "But I do not have much money."

"Then I will sell you one piece," Maria said. She

removed a pie from the wagon, set it on the sidewalk, and cut out one slice. Then she tore a sheet of paper towel off the roll and wrapped the slice of pie. Maria took the woman's money, handed her the piece of ah-play pee-ay, and continued on her way. Maria walked all the way across Acarigua, selling her ah-play pee-ay slice by slice, pie by pie.

When the pies were all gone, Ms. Walker asked Maria, "Now what are you going to do?"

"Now I will go home to Mama," Maria said, her pockets bulging with money. "And tomorrow I will get up with the sun to go buy the wood we need for our new house. It will be our ah-play pee-ay house, because I made all the money from ah-play pee-ays."

Ms. Walker laughed.

"You think I am funny?" Maria frowned. "You think I am stupid?"

"No," Ms. Walker assured her. "I think you are about the smartest girl I have ever met. I am the stupid one. When you said you were going to build an ah-play pee-ay house, I was afraid that you would try to stack the pies to make the walls."

"*That* is stupid!" Maria laughed. "You can't *build* a house out of ah-play pee-ays! But you can *make* a house from ah-play pee-ays. Just you wait and see. We will have the only ah-play pee-ay house in Acarigua."

Maria worked hard on the ah-play pee-ay house. She wanted to stay home from school, but her mother said no. As soon as classes ended, Maria would run to help build the house. All the family's friends helped, too. Maria bought wood for the frame, and the men put it up on the new land. The women patted mud into blocks and dried them in the sun. In three days the blocks were ready to be set in place. Even the children helped, slapping mud onto the walls to hold the blocks together. By the end of the third day, the house was finished.

"*Señora,* come with me today," Maria said to Ms. Walker after school, pulling on her hand. Together they went to Maria's new home. There, on the once-empty lot, stood a brand-new mud-brick house.

"It is wonderful!" Ms. Walker said, as proud of Maria as if she were her own daughter. "I will be right back," she called, hurrying away.

She soon came running back, all out of breath, and she handed Maria a small brown paper bag. "Open it," she said.

Maria peeked inside the bag and saw the shiny crystal apple from Ms. Walker's grandmother.

"Oh, *Señora!*" she exclaimed. "I can't take this."

"But I want you to have it," Ms. Walker insisted. She stepped inside the house and set the apple on the front window ledge.

"Now it is really an ah-play pee-ay house!" Maria said, smiling proudly.

"And it is the finest ah-play pee-ay house I have ever seen!" said Ms. Walker.

Mai's Magic

AN ORIGINAL STORY BY JASON SANFORD

Thai Words:

Prik: a very spicy pepper

Baht (pronounced "baht"): Thai money. One American dollar
   is equal to about twenty-five baht.

Sawatdee (pronounced "sa-wa-DEE"): means "hello."

In Thailand, some villages specialized in one prod-
uct—one village produced leather goods that were
used throughout the country, another was famous for
its knives. And the best gold jewelry came from the
tiny village of Ban Tawng.

In every shop, on every shelf, golden rings and
bracelets twinkled at passersby. People stared and said
every piece was perfect—a golden dream. Every piece,

that is, except the ones Aran Manit made.

Aran was a horrible goldsmith. His necklaces scratched people's necks, and babies cried when they looked at his bracelets. He kept hoping he would improve. His daughter, Mai, knew better.

"Father," she said, holding up his latest creation, "rings are supposed to be round, not triangular. When will you stop abusing gold and open a restaurant?"

Like most daughters Mai knew what her father really enjoyed. He loved cooking; he made the tastiest, hottest curry in the village. Unfortunately, he was determined to succeed as a goldsmith, not as a cook.

"Daughter, everyone in Ban Tawng is a goldsmith. Morning, noon, and night they hammer away at gold. Why should I be any different?"

"Because," Mai said, "bad goldsmiths don't make money, but good cooks do—especially in a village where people are so busy hammering that they never have time to cook."

Mai's father ignored her and started hammering at his gold ring. With the second swing he hit his thumb. "Ow-ow-owee!" Mai's father wailed, hopping around and holding his smashed thumb. Mai shook her head.

"Keep making gold rings," Mai said. "But we are

almost out of money. Will you agree that if you can't sell any jewelry in the next two weeks, you will try opening a restaurant?"

Mai's father thought about that. Ever since his wife had died, he'd wanted to honor her memory. She had been the best goldsmith in Ban Tawng. While she made jewelry, he ran the store, and together they had been the perfect team. Aran knew he lacked his wife's talent, but he was afraid to change jobs. However, he didn't want his only daughter to starve, either.

"Very well, daughter, two weeks," he said. Mai and her father smiled on the deal.

That night Aran tossed and turned, unable to sleep. He couldn't break his word to his daughter, but he was terrified at the thought of opening a restaurant. What if people laughed at him? There had to be a way to keep his shop open. If people wouldn't buy his gold rings because they were beautiful, maybe he could find another way to sell them. He had to think of *something*.

The next day, Mai came home from school to find a new sign in front of her father's shop: "Magic Charms for Sale. Magically Multiply Your Money!"

Mai groaned. Her father would do anything to

keep his gold store open—even lie. She hoped he had bad luck selling his fake charms.

Unknown to Mai, someone else was thinking about bad luck, too. His name was Lek and he was a thief.

"I can't believe how unlucky we are," Lek said. "I thought I taught you never to pick a pocket when someone is watching."

Lek's partner, a small brown monkey, winced. The monkey was specially trained to steal money. They had been traveling by train when the monkey stole a sleeping man's wallet. Unfortunately, a police officer saw them, and they had to jump off the speeding train to escape. They'd landed right in a stinky pool of mud. Lek had been forced to walk all night to his home in Ban Tawng. The monkey sat on his shoulder.

Lek was tired of stealing a little money here and there; he wanted to steal lots of money at once and be rich. The problem was that places with lots of money, like banks, were closely guarded. He didn't want to get killed robbing a bank. As Lek wondered what to do he saw a sign that said, "Magically Multiply Your Money!"

Lek smiled as a plan unfolded in his head. Soon he would be rich.

When Aran opened his store the next morning, a

crowd gathered outside the shop window. All day, people pointed at the sign and laughed. But no one bought Aran's magic rings. People said that the only thing the ugly rings would multiply was the number of people who laughed at you.

Later, Mai asked her father to give up his scheme.

"It's not a scheme," Aran said. "Please hand me some more peppers."

He was cooking spicy curry. Mai handed him the peppers, and he dumped them into the cooking pot. It was a hot day and flies were buzzing everywhere.

"My rings *are* magic," Mai's father insisted.

"It is dishonest," Mai said, brushing away a fly. "There are no such things as magic rings. You are lying to people."

"Prove that they aren't magic," her father said. Right then a large fly landed on his nose, and he swatted it. Instantly he shouted out and ran to the water jar, splashing water in his eyes.

"Are you okay, Father?" Mai asked. Her father had made a common cooking mistake. *Prik* peppers were so spicy that even after wiping off your hands, their residue would burn if you touched your eyes.

"Maybe the peppers are magic," Mai joked, "and

they are telling you not to lie about your rings."

Before she could say anything more, a bell chimed downstairs. Someone was in the gold shop. Mai's father went to see who it was.

"If Father would just open a restaurant," Mai thought, "everything would be fine. People know he is a great cook and would surely buy his curry. He just hates to admit defeat."

Mai heard her father talking downstairs, then the door chimes ringing as someone left. The steps creaked loudly as Aran ran upstairs.

"Look, Daughter, someone bought one of my charms," he shouted excitedly. "It was Lek."

Mai looked out the window as Lek walked down the dusty road that lead to the market. "Why would a thief buy a fake magic ring?" Mai wondered.

"Please excuse me, Father," Mai said. She ran after Lek to see what he was up to.

She followed him through the market to a fruit stand, where Lek asked to buy an orange. He reached into his pocket and suddenly jumped up, holding a wad of money thicker than a brick.

"It's true!" Lek shouted. "Look, I just bought one of Aran's magic rings and my money magically increased in my pocket."

A crowd of people pressed in, looking excitedly at Lek's money.

Mai was shocked.

"This isn't right," she said. "This man is a thief. He probably stole the money from one of us."

The villagers nodded at this; they knew Lek was a thief. Yet a quick check of the village found that no one was missing any money.

"I have no reason to lie," Lek said, waving his money. "Look at my money!"

Mai went home disgusted.

For the next few days Mai's father was very busy making and selling his magic rings. All of the villagers wanted them because money kept appearing in the pockets of people who wore the rings.

Mai was suspicious, so she followed Lek one morning as he walked through the market. Soon enough she saw him give his monkey some money.

Lek pointed to a woman wearing one of the magic rings. The monkey sneaked over to the woman and silently slipped the money into her pocket. Shortly afterward the woman was jumping up and down. "It's magic!" she shouted, waving her newfound baht.

No one noticed the little monkey climbing up Lek's leg. It took a piece of candy from his pocket as a reward and grinned at Mai.

"He's trained his monkey to pick pockets," Mai thought. "I bet he's planting leftover money from his last heist. I must tell someone."

Mai went to her teacher at school, figuring that he would trust her. But the teacher only laughed.

"How can a monkey pick pockets?" the teacher asked. "You have an overactive imagination." Mai walked away dejected.

"I'll just have to show people what Lek is doing," she thought.

The next day Mai found Lek standing around the market.

"*Sawatdee,* Lek," Mai said. "May I pet your monkey?"

"Sure," Lek said. He noticed a magic ring on Mai's finger. "Have you gotten any magic money yet?" he asked.

"Not yet," Mai said. She pulled a piece of candy from her pocket and gave it to the monkey, who chewed it up then begged for more. Mai shook her head, and the monkey threw a temper tantrum.

"I guess he likes my candy," Mai said. She walked

over to a bench, sat down, and pretended to read a book.

"Lek will tell his monkey to put money in my pocket," she thought. "If I believe in the magic everyone in the village will trust him."

Sure enough, out of the corner of her eye Mai saw the little monkey sneak away from Lek. Mai kept very still and felt a slight stirring in her pocket. "Smart monkey," she thought. Her extra candy was in that pocket. The monkey planned to do two things at once: steal some candy and plant the money.

Mai smiled. The candy in her pocket was extra-special. When the monkey was gone, she turned around to watch Lek. The monkey sat on his shoulder, holding the stolen candy.

The little monkey bit into the candy and started chewing. Immediately his face went red and he screeched. Mai had smeared the candy in her pocket with *prik*-pepper sauce. The monkey jumped into a water jar and drank madly while the villagers stared.

"Looks like Lek's monkey doesn't like the candy it stole from my pocket," Mai said so everyone could hear.

"Nonsense," Lek shouted, seeing Mai's trap. "You fed my monkey that peppered candy just to be cruel."

"No I didn't. That monkey stole the candy from my pocket."

"Now, who are you going to believe?" Lek asked the villagers around him. "A little girl or a grown man?"

People nodded at this. "Mai must be imagining things," someone said. "No monkey can pick pockets."

Mai walked home angry but determined. "Next time," she thought, "I will prove to everyone that he is a liar and a thief."

For the next two days, no more money magically appeared in anyone's pockets, which upset people with a ring. Lek told everyone that this was because the magic had grown old and weak.

"I have had much experience with magic during my travels," Lek said. "Once magic disappears, it is gone forever. We must take advantage of the remaining magic before it is gone."

The villagers agreed. They'd benefited from the magic, and didn't want it to stop. Lek suggested that Mai's father make a super-ring to focus the remaining magic.

"We can put everyone's money in one place," Lek said. "We'll leave it there overnight so the ring has time to muster up its remaining magic. Then, come morning, we will all be rich."

The villagers liked Lek's idea. Mai's father especially loved the plan because it relied on his skills as a goldsmith.

"You can even put the money in my store overnight," Aran offered.

Mai knew that this was what Lek wanted. As soon as all the money in the village was in one place, his monkey would steal it. She had to stop him.

That evening the villagers carried all their money to Aran's store. Even Lek brought his stolen money.

"He wants to divert suspicion away from himself," Mai thought. "If his money disappears along with everyone else's, then people will think he is innocent and instead blame my father."

Everyone was excited at the prospect of becoming rich and eagerly touched the giant ring that Aran had made. Mai ignored the ring and instead watched Lek. His monkey was jumping all over the shop, looking at the space under the door, at the air vents on the walls. "He's figuring out how to sneak in," Mai realized. But she didn't worry. She had a big surprise ready.

The money was placed in an empty water jar that stood five feet tall. Mai's father wrote down how much money each family gave. When everyone's money was in the jar, Mai walked over to it.

"Let me pack the money down so it will have more room to increase," she said. Mai pushed the money down, then closed the lid.

"Let us now go to bed," Aran told the villagers. "The money will be safe here. My windows are barred and I will bolt the door from inside. No one will be able to break in and steal our money."

"But a small monkey can slip between the bars on the windows," Mai thought. However, she said nothing. Everyone went to sleep and dreamed greedy dreams. Mai didn't dream, but she slept soundly, confident that she had things under control.

The next day, the village awoke at dawn and gathered outside Aran's gold shop. When Aran opened his shop, the villagers crowded around the money jar.

"This is it," Mai's father said happily. He lifted the jar's lid, looked down, then quickly slammed the lid shut. He face went pale as everybody shouted at him to show them their money.

"Daughter," Aran whispered with fright. "I'm in big trouble."

The jar was empty!

"He stole the money," Lek shouted. "My money was in the jar, just like yours. I trusted Aran, and now I am poor."

The villagers yelled at Aran. "Where is our money, thief? We trusted you! How could you deceive us?"

Mai let this go on for a minute. Then she shouted, "I know where the money is." Slowly everyone quieted down to listen to her.

Mai continued, "There never was any magic, but there is a thief and I can prove it. It's very simple: the thief will not be able to touch his eyes."

Mai touched her eyes, followed by her father. All the villagers wanted to prove that they were not thieves. One by one they touched their eyes then looked around, curious. Mai waited, staring at Lek.

Lek touched his eyes. For a moment he paused, then he leapt up screaming. The monkey jumped from his shoulder as Lek clutched his head, tears streaming down his red face.

"When I packed the money down yesterday I dumped *prik* pepper powder all over it," Mai said. "The monkey slipped between the window bars, stole the money, and gave it to Lek, who got the powder all over his hands."

The villagers grabbed Lek. His eyes were so red and puffy, he could barely see. In exchange for water to wash his eyes with, he told all. The money was buried in a nearby rice field. He had planned to accuse Aran of stealing the money, then dig it up when the excitement died down.

That evening, Mai's father served up some of the hottest, tastiest curry he had ever made. Tears were streaming down Mai's face, but the curry was so good, she kept eating.

"Does this mean you will finally open a restaurant?" Mai asked.

"I have no choice," her father said. "Our neighbors said that if I ever touch gold again they would throw me out of the village. They also said I should heed my daughter's advice, because no one in the village is smarter than she."

Mai smiled. She petted Lek's monkey, who was living with them while Lek was in prison.

"I'm glad I won't have to hear you hammering your thumbs anymore," Mai said. "Now, could I please have a little more curry? With extra peppers!"

Author Biographies

Sandy Cudmore grew up on a cotton farm in Mississippi with her parents and four brothers. She spent all her free time riding horses, swimming, and water skiing. She now lives in Southern California and has two grown sons. Always an animal lover, Sandy has three big dogs and two iguanas (one is five feet long) and she raises desert tortoises. Sandy is a preschool teacher, and has cotaught Early Childhood Education classes at U.C.L.A., Ext. She went to college at Mississippi State, University of Georgia, and U.C.L.A. Her articles and short stories have been published in *T.E.A.M.* and *Animal Tales* magazines. Her story, "Fishing for Trouble," is original.

Laurie Eynon has worked with kids of all ages for many years as an English teacher and as the Director of Youth Ministry at a Presbyterian Church in Columbus, Indiana, where she lives. Laurie has two grown sons—one a real-estate developer and the other a fish biologist. She enjoys tennis, travel, reading, movies, and theater, and writes for a number of magazines. Laurie is an aspiring playwright, with an off-Broadway production to her credit. Her story, "Save Wellington Woods!!," is original.

J.M. Kelly is the author of a number of books for children, including a biography of Benjamin Franklin and an adaptation of stories by Washington Irving. He lives in New York's Hudson Valley, the scene of Irving's famous tale "Rip Van Winkle." Kelly is a volunteer with his local fire department and has written about the history of ambulances. He has written about business and history for many magazines, and he has a story in *Girls to the Rescue, Book #3*. His story, "Keesha and the Rat," is original.

Bruce Lansky enjoys writing funny poems for children (the most popular of which are in *Poetry Party, Kids Pick the Funniest Poems, A Bad Case of the Giggles, No More Homework! No More Tests!*, and *New Adventures of Mother Goose*), and he loves to perform in school assemblies and workshops. Before he started to write children's books, Lansky wrote humorous books for parents and baby name books. He has two grown children and currently lives with his computer near a beautiful lake in Minnesota. His story, "Temper, Temper," is adapted from Italian folklore.

Liya Lev Oertel is originally from Minsk, Byelorussia, and she based her story, "Rachel's Promise," on a true event that happened to her grandmother. Liya graduated from Brown University with degrees in psychology and visual arts. Currently, she works as an editor and lives in Minneapolis, Minnesota, with her husband, Jens. Liya has a story published in *Newfangled Fairy Tales, Book #1*. She loves mysteries, gardening, dancing, and swimming.

Jason Sanford has just returned from Thailand, where he taught English for two years as a Peace Corps Volunteer. Before going overseas, Jason worked as a lifeguard at Walt Disney World, a newspaper reporter in Tuskegee, Alabama, and an archeologist for Auburn University. He currently lives in Minneapolis, Minnesota, with his wife, Jennifer, who was also a Peace Corps Volunteer in Thailand. Jason's story, "Mai's Magic," is based on his experiences with the little spicy peppers that grow in Thailand.

Janet Elaine Smith is a contributing editor to *Heritage Magazine,* has a column in *Red River Valley Memories* magazine, and has had articles published in many other magazines. Janet has also published three books: *Digging in the Dirt, Tickling Your Ancestral Funny Bone,* and *A Hallet History.* She teaches genealogy (tracing your family history) and is president of the Minnkota Genealogical Society. Janet lives in Grand Forks, North Dakota, with her husband, Ivan, and has three grown children. Janet and her husband lived in Venezuela, South America, for several years. That experience served as the inspiration for her story "The Apple Pie House."

Diane Sawyer's stories have appeared in newspapers, magazines, and journals, including the *St. Petersburg Times, Writers' International Forum,* and *Arts & Letters.* She belongs to the Writers' Round Table—a three-member critiquing group—and attends writing workshops and seminars. When not participating in tennis, swimming, and other fitness activities, Diane enjoys spending time with her husband, Robert, and children. Her story, "Skateboard Rosie and the Soda Kids," is original.

Girls to the Rescue

Edited by Bruce Lansky

A collection of ten folk- and fairy tales featuring courageous, clever, and determined girls from around the world. When girls see this collection they will say, "Finally! We get to be the heroes." As Lansky brought nursery rhymes into the 1990s with his bestseller *The New Adventures of Mother Goose*, this groundbreaking book updates traditional fairy tales for girls ages 7 to 13.

Order # 2215 $3.95

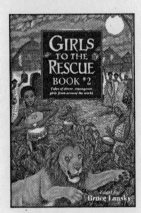

Girls to the Rescue, Book #2

Edited by Bruce Lansky

Here is the second groundbreaking collection of folktales featuring ten clever and courageous girls from around the world. You will meet Jamila, a girl who saves her village from a terrible lion; Adrianna, a Mexican girl who rescues her family's farm from ruin; and Vassilisa, a Russian aristocrat who saves her brother from prison. (Ages 7 to 13)

Order # 2216 $3.95

Girls to the Rescue, Book #3

Edited by Bruce Lansky

The runaway success of the *Girls to the Rescue* series continues with this third collection of folktales from around the world, featuring such heroic girls as Emily, a girl who helps a runaway slave and her baby daughter reach safety and freedom; Sarah, a Polish girl who saves her father from prison; and Kamala, a Punjabi girl who outsmarts a pack of thieves. (Ages 7 to 13)

Order # 2219 $3.95

Young Marian's Adventures in Sherwood Forest

by Stephen Mooser

In the tradition of *Girls to the Rescue,* the popular series of short-story anthologies featuring girls as heroes, this novel-length story tells the exciting tale of spunky, 13-year-old Maid Marian. With the help of young Robin of Loxely, the future Robin Hood, Marian battles a pack of hungry wolves and outsmarts murderous thieves and the Sheriff of Nottingham while trying to save her father from the hangman's noose and solve the mystery of her missing mother.

Order # 2218 $4.50

Throw a *Girls to the Rescue* Party!

We have created a *Girls to the Rescue* event kit that we make available to bookstores and schools. The kit includes fun activities, bookmarks, and buttons for all participants. If you want to have a *Girls to the Rescue* party, contact your local bookstore and ask them to set one up. And if you want to have a *Girls to the Rescue* party at school, have your teacher contact our Promotion Manager by using the address on the order form in the back of this book or call 1-800-338-2232.

Perform a *Girls to the Rescue* Play!

Now you can produce *Girls to the Rescue* plays at school using scripts and materials from Baker Plays. Have your teacher contact Baker Plays at (617) 482-1280 for more information.

Newfangled Fairy Tales, Book #1

Edited by Bruce Lansky

This is a collection of ten delightful fairy tales with new twists on old stories and themes, including:

- a contemporary King Midas who doesn't have time for his son's Little League games,

- a prince who refuses to marry any of the unpleasant, grumpy, and complaining young women who had slept on mattresses with peas under them,

- a beautiful princess who was put to sleep for 100 years because she was so cranky,

- a clever princess who paid a dragon to lose a fight with a prince so she could marry the man she loved.

Order # 2500 $3.95

Order Form

Qty.	Title	Author	Order No.	Unit Cost (U.S. $)	Total
	Bad Case of the Giggles	Lansky, B.	2411	$15.00	
	Best Birthday Party Game Book	Lansky, B.	6064	$3.95	
	Free Stuff for Kids	Free Stuff Editors	2190	$5.00	
	Girls to the Rescue	Lansky, B.	2215	$3.95	
	Girls to the Rescue, Book #2	Lansky, B.	2216	$3.95	
	Girls to the Rescue, Book #3	Lansky, B.	2219 .	$3.95	
	Girls to the Rescue, Book #4	Lansky, B.	2221	$3.95	
	Just for Fun Party Game Book	Warner, P.	6065	$3.95	
	Kids Are Cookin'	Brown, K.	2440	$8.00	
	Kids Pick-A-Party Book	Warner, P.	6090	$9.00	
	Kids Pick the Funniest Poems	Lansky, B.	2410	$15.00	
	Kids' Holiday Fun	Warner, P.	6000	$12.00	
	Kids' Party Cookbook	Warner, P.	2435	$12.00	
	Kids' Party Games and Activities	Warner, P.	6095	$12.00	
	New Adventures of Mother Goose	Lansky, B.	2420	$15.00	
	Newfangled Fairy Tales	Lansky, B.	2500	$3.95	
	No More Homework! No More Tests!	Lansky, B.	2414	$8.00	
	Poetry Party	Lansky, B.	2430	$12.00	
	Young Marian's Adventures	Mooser, S.	2218	$4.50	
				Subtotal	
		Shipping and Handling, see below			
		MN residents add 6.5% sales tax			
				Total	

YES, please send me the books indicated above. Add $2.00 shipping and handling for the first book and $.50 for each additional book. Add $2.50 to total for books shipped to Canada. Overseas postage will be billed. Allow up to four weeks for delivery. Send check or money order payable to Meadowbrook Press. No cash or C.O.D.'s please. Prices subject to change without notice. **Quantity discounts available upon request.**

Send book(s) to:

Name _____

Address _____

City _____ State _____ Zip _____

Telephone (_____) _____

Purchase order number (if necessary) _____

Payment via:

☐ Check or money order payable to Meadowbrook (No cash or C.O.D.'s please)
   Amount enclosed $ _____

☐ Visa (for orders over $10.00 only)   ☐ MasterCard (for orders over $10.00 only)

Account # _____

Signature _____ Exp. Date _____

You can also phone us for orders of $10.00 or more at 1-800-338-2232.

A *FREE* Meadowbrook catalog is available upon request.

Mail to: Meadowbrook Press
5451 Smetana Drive, Minnetonka, MN 55343

Phone (612) 930-1100   Toll-Free 1-800-338-2232   Fax (612) 930-1940